"If I die young, bury me

My therapist would agree, c

mechanism. "Lay me down

I felt a bead of perspi

smack-dab between my breasts.

This year's Thanksgiving dinner with your roommate's family is brought to you by boob sweat.

The sooner I got into this air-conditioned house, the better. I jostled the potatoes to one hip so I could ring the doorbell, which was inconveniently offset to the side of the door and behind a potted plant. Alas, my denim shorts and cropped tee were no match for the scalding casserole dish. Could I have set the dish down on the ground to ring the doorbell? Of course. Did I? Absolutely not. My stubborn Aries self would never allow such a choice.

Instead, I glanced behind me to make sure that nobody was around to witness the humiliation I was about to subject myself to. Thankfully, the cul-de-sac was empty. No doubt everybody on Sutter Canyon Road was already enjoying their Thanksgiving dinner and football. Coast now clear, I craned my body around Geoff's thriving Monstera plant, making a quick mental note to ask him for gardening tips later.

I engaged my core as I balanced on one leg, and sent up a "Hail Mary!" to my yoga teacher (who ironically, was a drag queen named Mary, Queen of Thots). I carefully dodged the "I Yam Thankful" flag, no doubt something Genie had picked up on sale at Target, before bending until the tip of my nose was even with the doorbell. Without giving it a second thought, I leaned forward and pressed my nose to the bell.

I could practically hear Mary now. *"Flawless Warrior Three, Nora,"* she'd say.

A chime echoed through the house, along with a dog's bark. It didn't take long for Genie to open the door.

"Nora, I'm so glad you could make it. We were worried we'd miss you this year, sweetie," she said, gesturing me (and the potatoes) inside.

"Thank you for having me. As always."

I'd known Genie and Geoff almost as long as I'd known my roommate, Riley. We'd met during junior year of college and bonded over the fact that we were both from the San Fernando Valley and yet, had somehow never met until attending school together... in Washington state. That and we both hated avocados.

Genie guided me towards the kitchen at the backend of the house. I'd spent countless holidays, graduation parties, and family dinners at the Miller house, but even a stranger would have no trouble finding the kitchen on a day like today. Where else could that delicious aroma of buttery, carb-filled goodness be coming from?

Thanks to my latest gig, I'd been a last-minute addition to this year's festivities. After I insisted on contributing something to our meal – four or five times, I might add – Genie had finally relented and said that I could bring the potatoes. That was perfectly fine with me. Truly, I believed the potatoes were the best part of every Thanksgiving.

"Ri told us you're starring in a movie. That's amazing!" She fiddled around the kitchen, gathering supplies for dinner.

I sighed. "Thank you, but I'm not sure I'd call *Cam Girl #4* in a USC short film a 'starring' role."

"Nonsense. Better than *Cam Girl #5*, right?" She winked. I only wished my parents understood (or supported) my career choice as much as Genie.

"Now be honest, Genie." I tilted my head to one side and put on my best faux-lecturing voice. One that I usually reserved for the kiddos I nannied. "Are you excited to see me, or... the potatoes?" I pulled back

Meet Me in Los Feliz

a hot holiday novella

Kelly Reynolds

Cover Design and Illustration by Julie Olivia

Contents

Author's Note

Meet Me in Los Feliz is a low-angst, high-on-the-holidays (in more ways than one) romance novella. This book can be read as a stand-alone. There are no cliffhangers.

Please be advised that this book is an **open-door** romance, meaning there is **on-page, explicit** sexual content (between consenting adults), including oral sex, vaginal and anal penetration, toy play, light bondage, and choking. There's also recreational use of alcohol and marijuana. Mature readers only.

The holidays are stressful for so many of us, which is why this book is pure sex and shenanigans. It pairs best with a mug of boozy hot chocolate and your favorite adult toy. Cheers.

*For all the fat queens, short kings, and the people **lucky** enough to fall in love with us.*

Chapter One

Thanksgiving Day

Nora

There's nothing quite like standing on somebody's front porch in 92-degree heat while clutching a bowl of mashed potatoes.

Garlic and goat cheese mashed potatoes, to be exact – about as bougie as mashed potatoes can get. Then again, you'd be hard-pressed to find something non-bougie about Los Angeles these days. From the "Saved by the Bell" pop-ups to the Museum of Broken Relationships (which I'd proudly contributed to, so take that Evan Jacobson, you douche nozzle) and $10 CBD lattes, LA had practically cornered the market on all things bougie. And I knew that better than most. I was one of the few who could call themselves a born and bred Angeleno, which was more of a rarity than people might expect.

The combined heat and weight of the casserole dish began to make me sweat.

the casserole dish lid with a flourish, releasing a cloud of steam and the mouth-watering smell of garlic.

Mm, smells like... nobody's getting laid tonight.

Not that anybody ever felt like having sex after Thanksgiving dinner, but as the resident single person of my friend group, it only seemed fair. If I wasn't getting stuffed after stuffing, neither were you.

"Those smell amazing," Genie said. "I'll grab another serving spoon. Why don't you go ahead and set them out on the table? Ri and Dev's plane was delayed on their way back from Cancun, I haven't even heard from Kendall today so who knows where she's at, and the food's going to get cold if we wait any longer. So, let's just dig in without them!"

Riley had texted me earlier that morning to let me know that her and Devin's flight had been delayed. As much as I loved my roommates, I'd been somewhat relieved as their delay had given me enough time to clean up the mess I'd made of our place. Well, *their* place, really. They'd bought the North Hollywood townhouse two years ago and graciously invited me to live there with them. At the time, the three of us had already been living together, but even then, I knew them buying a place as a couple meant a step forward in their relationship. One that would slightly alter our living environment. Ever since we'd moved into the townhouse, I'd felt more like a house guest than a roommate. And unfortunately, I was not the tidiest house guest.

Case in point, I'd spent the morning picking up empty chip bags, dirty coffee mugs, and bras. Because what grown ass woman didn't remove her bra the moment she got home? I just had a nasty habit of flinging my bras anywhere and everywhere.

Seeing as I'd been filming most of the week and nannying in between, I'd barely had a chance to miss my roommates. I was glad they'd be back tonight, although judging by Genie's frustration, it wouldn't be soon enough. And it was much easier to blame her daughter for throwing off her Thanksgiving timetable, than to blame Jet Blue.

"Genie, I'm going to use the restroom really quick," I said, already backing away towards the hall bathroom.

"Oh, use Kendall and Riley's bathroom. The downstairs toilet has been making a funny noise all week."

I changed course and hustled up the stairs towards the hall bathroom, but only after removing my boots. It was more than obvious that Genie already had a lot on her mind. The last thing she needed was a dirty carpet. I passed Geoff on my way up the stairs, who in typical dad fashion, thought it'd be hilarious to act like we were going to run into each other. He pumped to the left and faked to the right, adding a "woah, woah" with each exaggerated move.

"Happy Thanksgiving, Geoff. I'll be down in a second." He patted my back and I brushed by him. Not in a creepy way, but rather an *"Alright, kiddo"* kind of tone. Considering he was a retired college football coach, I much preferred the cheesy dad jokes and back pats to any gruff, ass-slapping. I didn't even like having my ass slapped during sex.

I shoved the bathroom door open, never expecting to find anybody on the other side. The freckle-faced, ginger hottie with his dick in his hands stopped me cold.

Well, I guess this year, I have something else to be thankful for.

Bowie

Growing up with two mums had certainly had its advantages. Healthy emotional parenting, well-planned holidays, and an in-depth, shame-free education about "how to be a generous lover" in my teen years. However, one thing they'd failed to cover was how to properly respond when somebody barges in on you in the loo while your cock's out. Speaking of my cock...

Bloody hell.

I turned away from the purple-haired goddess – because even though I'd only caught a quick peek, I knew that a woman with curves like that deserved to be worshipped – and tucked myself back into my trousers. I zipped up and flushed the toilet. Glancing over, I found the beautiful intruder utterly slack-jawed, still staring at my crotch. "Sorry, do you mind?"

Her eyes lifted to meet mine. They were the perfect shade of my favorite English Breakfast tea, two sugars, one milk, just the way I liked it. It might've made for an odd comparison to the average bloke, but not to a Brit and certainly not to this Brit who owned a tearoom.

"Oh my god. I'm so sorry!" She simultaneously covered her eyes and turned to flee. I wasn't about to let her blindly tumble down the stairs though.

"Hey, it's no problem." Her steps halted. She kept her eyes covered though and turned away from me. Such a shame, although I can't say I was upset with the view from behind. The denim shorts she wore didn't leave much to the imagination, except maybe a tattoo or two. What I wouldn't give to trace those tattoos (preferably with my tongue) and see where they led.

Woah, Bo. Getting ahead of yourself, aren't you?

"Do you mind if I ask who you are?"

Without removing her hands from her face, she turned back towards me. Well, sort of. She ended up facing the linen closet just outside the bathroom. "Nora. I'm Riley and Devin's roommate. At least I was, before I died. Just now."

My lips curved up. "It's fine, I promise. I'm Bowie. And I'm uh, contained now." She reluctantly opened her eyes, first one and then the other, before slowly pulling her hands away from her face. Until it was just the two of us facing one another, me still inside the loo, and her just beyond the doorway.

"Bowie?" I liked how she said my name, the way the "B" vibrated from her lips. Even more so, I liked the way her lips puckered when she said it. I imagined they'd look the same way when she kissed. "Oh!" Surprise registered across her face. "You're Kendall's boyfriend?"

"Er, yeah."

When Kendall had invited me to her family's Thanksgiving last week, I'd been shocked to say the least. Apparently, she hadn't told them we'd broken up... almost a month ago. She'd asked me to play the doting boyfriend role for the holiday and I'd agreed. It's not as if I'd had plans of my own. Plus, our break-up had been amicable – a little dull, really – so I hadn't questioned it. What I wasn't excited about was the fact that she'd deserted me at her family's house.

But that wasn't my story to tell. Not to Kendall's family and not to Nora. No matter how much I bloody well wanted to.

"Riley's told me all about you. It's nice to finally meet." She took a step forward, palm now raised for a handshake. I lifted mine up and gestured to the sink. "Right. Well, I'll just let you..." she trailed off.

"I'll be done in a second. I'm assuming you need the toilet?" She smirked, no doubt laughing at my "Briticism". That's what my employees called them.

I quickly washed up and dried my hands. "All yours." I had to walk around her on my way out of the room, which brought us practically side-by-side. Even if it was only for a second or two. That's all I needed to notice that she was taller than most women. Then again, I was shorter than most men. Not short, by any means, but 5'8" on a good day (5'7" at the doctor's office). Nora had at least a couple inches on me, but that didn't matter. If anything, it only added to her goddess-like figure, rich in abundant, soft curves.

She thinks you're in a relationship, you twat. Stop staring.

I left her to her business and headed downstairs. Just as my feet hit the final step, Genie rounded the corner into the dining room, arms loaded with dishes, cutlery, and... was that a pie? "May I help you, Mrs. Miller?"

"Bowie, honey, it's Genie," she chastised. "And why don't you grab the plates? I've decided we're not waiting for my delinquent children any longer." I carefully extricated the dishes from her arms and together, we set the table. "You haven't heard from Kendall, have you?"

"Umm..."

"Because she should've been here over an hour ago."

"Right..."

"I just figured the two of you would drive over together." My grip faltered. One of the plates clanked onto the table harder than I would've hoped. "Careful honey," she said. "We bought those during a trip to the Turks and Caicos. It was a very long flight. I would hate to have to go back, just to replace one of the plates."

While I hoped she was just taking the piss, I couldn't be sure. In the few times I'd met Genie, I'd never been able to gauge Genie's sense of humor (or if she even had one).

Not ten minutes later, we all sat down to dinner. *All* meaning Genie, who was now on her second bottle of Merlot, Geoff, who'd insisted on carving the turkey with a "real knife" rather than the electric carver, Nora, and me. Best not forget the empty places reserved for Riley, her partner, Devin, and of course, Kendall, who hadn't responded to any of my texts this afternoon.

"Excellent cook on the bird, Geoff." Nora smiled around a mouthful of turkey.

"Did you try the brussels sprouts? I used the air fryer *Rivin* got me for Christmas." Genie and Nora both murmured their appreciation. Geoff must've sensed my confusion because he explained, "Riley and Devin. *Rivin* is their couple's name. You know, like *Brangelina*..."

"They broke up," Nora pointed out.

"Or Kimye..."

"Them too," she retorted.

"Jethroux."

Nora paused. "Who's that?"

"Jennifer Anniston and Justin Theroux," Geoff responded, never missing a beat.

"Oh, good one." She forked together another piece of gravy-soaked turkey. "Sadly, they called it quits, too."

"Damn it. Is nothing sacred anymore?"

"Honey." Genie rested her hand on Geoff's arm. "Maybe this is a sign that you shouldn't 'celebrity couple name' your daughters' relationships." She turned to me. "He gets all his news from *Us Weekly*."

Nora's eyes caught mine and she swallowed. I felt my lips lift in return. I couldn't be certain, but her cheeks might've pinkened as well. Was it me or the tryptophan that had her blushing?

"Bowie, I keep meaning to come to your shop." I reluctantly turned my focus away from Nora and towards Genie. "I just know my book club would love to meet there sometime. Tea and scones and books, oh my!" She chuckled. I guess she did have a sense of humor... sort of. Then again, I'd always thought people who laughed at their own jokes were the worst.

"You're welcome anytime. On the house, of course."

"Oh, aren't you the sweetest? Kendall better hang onto you." This time I was the one blushing, and not in a good way.

"What's the name?" Nora asked. This was the first time she'd spoken directly to me since the toilet exchange.

"Sorry?" I must've missed the first part of her question.

"Your shop. It's a tearoom, yeah?"

"Yes, Althea's. In Los Feliz."

When Nan bought the property over a decade ago, she'd truly lucked out with the location. Since her passing, it'd taken a bit of luck, a smidge of fate, and a fuck-ton of the money I'd inherited from her to keep the business afloat. I loved my nan, but she hadn't been the best bookkeeper. Thankfully, Althea's was finally in the black.

"And are you, Althea?" *Damn.* Thick, tattooed, and cheeky? Nora was my kind of woman.

"No," I smiled. "That would be my nan."

"*Kenwie.*" Geoff exclaimed.

"Sorry?" I asked. I'd almost forgotten that we weren't alone.

"That's your celebrity couple name. You and Kendall," he explained. I could feel the heat creeping up my neck. Judging by Nora's furrowed brow, my discomfort was obvious. "*Kenwie* and *Rivin*. Honey, we should get them shirts for Christmas, and–"

"Speaking of *Rivin*..." Nora held up her phone. "Riley texted to say they should be here any minute." As if by divine intervention, the front door burst open. Only it wasn't Riley or Devin, but Kendall. My pretend-she's-not-your-ex ex-girlfriend.

"Happy Thanksgiving, family!" Kendall chirped her greeting completely unawares of the the fact that we'd begun dinner without her. Or that she was nearly two hours late. "Boy, have I got exciting news." She sat at one of the empty places and began to make herself a plate.

"Kendall. Louise. Miller. Where have you been?" Genie asked, venom edging each word in her daughter's name.

"Starving. Did you make grandma's cornbread?"

"If *somebody* wanted me to make grandma's cornbread, then *somebody* should've come by at two with the buttermilk that *somebody* said they would bring."

There was some American saying about killing with kindness instead of vinegar, or something like that. Whoever came up with that one hadn't been referring to Genie Miller. From what I could tell, Genie Miller killed with the closest sharp object and then poured vinegar on the open wound. And all with a pinched smile on her face.

"Whatever, it's not important." Kendall waved off the hypothetical cornbread. This was one of the reasons we'd ended our relationship after only four months. I'd been attracted to her outgoing personality and spontaneity at the start, but at the end of day, Kendall was only interested in Kendall. "What is important is my new job opportunity!" She practically vibrated out of her seat.

"That's brilliant," I said, before tacking on, "babe."

"Oh." Kendall's excitement waned when she noticed me for the first time. "Thanks Bowie."

"Kendall," Geoff interrupted. "We were talking about celebrity couple names and I decided that your name is–"

"I'm moving to Bali!" Kendall exclaimed. Silence descended on the dinner table. Nora and I filled the silence by taking generous sips of our wine.

"Excuse me?" Genie asked, feigning calm.

Maybe I tuned out the next couple of minutes of Kendall droning on about the yoga externship position she'd received in Bali. Maybe I blacked out. Maybe I'd accidentally had a bit more wine than I'd thought. Whatever the case, what I did notice was Nora. I noticed the way she'd tucked a piece of her shoulder-length hair behind her ear. And the fact that every time she'd lift her silverware, I'd catch a peek-a-boo of a bumblebee tattoo under her arm. I had so many questions I wanted to ask her and only one thing I wanted to tell her: that I was no longer dating her roommate's sister.

But all of that would have to wait until the screaming subsided.

"...And I don't understand, how could you do this to us? How could you do this to Bowie?" Genie shouted across the table.

"Bowie? Bowie and I broke up a month ago!" Kendall yelled back.

My knife and fork clattered to the plate. I sucked in a lungful of air and awaited the Millers' reactions.

"Then why did you invite him to Thanksgiving?!"

While the Millers hurled jabs around the table faster than balls at Wimbledon, I turned my focus to the woman sitting across from me. Nora's gaze met mine. Not knowing what else to do, let alone say, I subtly lifted and lowered my shoulders. She bit her lip to hide a smile. I could tell she wanted to say more but knew that this wasn't the time and place. Plus, nothing could've prepared any of us for what happened next when Riley and Devin burst through the front door.

"Mom, Dad, everybody!" She lifted her left hand, emphasizing the sparkling band on her fourth finger. "Devin and I got married in Cancun!!"

"What!?" Genie and Geoff both shouted.

A glass broke. Someone screamed. The dog howled. I don't know what I'd expected for my first American Thanksgiving, but this certainly wasn't it. This was better.

Chapter Two

December 1st

Nora

The door to Althea's Tearoom chimed as I held it wide for Olive and Sage. A burst of air-conditioning hit us the moment we crossed the threshold. It'd been an unseasonably hot fall thus far, though warmer temps in October and November weren't exactly rare for Southern California. The fact that we were all still rocking cutoffs and crop tops didn't surprise me. What was surprising was the winter wonderland that awaited inside Althea's Tearoom.

My mini sidekicks, also known as "my nanny kiddos", half-jumped, half-skipped into the storefront. There was nothing quite like little girl enthusiasm. I'd been nannying for Olive and Sage, who were eight and six respectively since Sage was in diapers. After years of chaperoning field trips, attending school orientations, and enduring countless ballet recitals (or CrossFit Kids competitions, in Sage's case), I could safely say that motherhood was not for me. That didn't mean I didn't love the heck out of the little boogers.

"Nora, look!" Sage exclaimed before making a beeline for a glass cabinet full of cakes and cookies. The kid has one hell of a sweet tooth, though who could blame her? Cake was delicious as fuck. Literally. I'd never met a man who could make me moan like a slice of cake.

Olive, who was eight-going-on-twenty-eight, clung to my side. Heaven forbid she show too much excitement for anything – even sweet treats. She was much "too cool" for that, something she reminded me and her parents of daily. I practically dragged her over to the counter.

"Why are their decorations already up? It's barely December." she asked, her eyes catching on the twinkle lights strung across the ceiling, end-to-end. And the festive décor didn't stop there. Hand-cut paper snowflakes of all shapes and sizes hung from the ceiling as well. The windows had been glazed with faux frost, a stark contrast to the outside heat. A large wreath, decked out in blue, silver, and white ornaments, decorated the space above the register. Even the overhead lights, which upon closer inspection, were overturned teacups wired with a bulb, had been trimmed with garland.

"Okay, Grinch," I said, sarcasm dripping from my mouth. "You got something against holiday cheer, Ollie?" I lightly nudged her shoulder.

"It's just... very bright and colorful."

"Of course, it is," a deep, familiar voice added from behind us.

All three of us turned to find Bowie leaning against the door frame to what I assumed was the kitchen, arms folded across his lean physique. The same physique that to my disappointment, was all covered up by a work apron. One adorned with snowflakes and mittens, because of course.

"I don't know about you lovely ladies, but where I come from, the holidays are full of colors. 'May your days be merry and...?'" He gestured to Sage and Olive.

"Bright!" Sage burst out. Olive's eyes narrowed. She looked seconds away from knocking the lopsided smile off Bowie's face. He clearly didn't know who he was messing with.

"That's right," he said. "Plus, the brighter the lights, the easier it is for Santa to find me, and I'm a long way from home. I don't want to miss out on any presents."

Olive rolled her eyes. I gave her shoulder a comforting squeeze. Smart kid that she was, I knew she wanted nothing more than to dive into some tirade about how Santa wasn't real, and it was meta-physically impossible for him to travel the globe in one-night, blah blah blah. She was definitely *that kid*. However, she was also a great sister and after several conversations with both me and her parents, she understood that it wasn't her place to "ruin the magic", so to speak, for Sage. Even though we weren't related, Olive took after me in that way. We were both realists, through-and-through.

"Santa only brings you presents if you've been nice," Sage told Bowie, very matter of fact.

Bowie sidled over to us before placing his hands on his waist. Did I spy a hint of biceps behind the Bohemian Rhapsody t-shirt? "Are you insinuating I've been naughty?" he taunted, sending Sage into a fit of giggles.

"Have you?" I asked.

His eyes bounced from Sage to me. "Have I what?"

"Been naughty?"

Bowie's brows raised, almost reaching the tips of his rust-colored curls. His lips parted, but no words came out. Just an exhalation of air.

You dumb bitch. Stop flirting with the hot Brit.

A relationship was the last thing on my mind these days. Although, truth be told, romance had always come second to my career aspirations. As I saw it, there'd be plenty of time for that later. Hollywood, on the other hand, did not take kindly to actresses over forty, much less fat actresses. No, my career opportunities had an expiration date, and the window was closing quickly.

There'd be plenty of time for British tea shop owners later. In the meantime, there were vibrators.

Great, now I'm thinking about what Bowie could do with a vibrator.

"Can I have cake *and* cookies, Nora?" Sage asked, intruding on the less than wholesome thoughts I'd been having about Bowie. Saved by the six-year-old.

"May I," I corrected her. "And no." She pouted, an adorable crease forming between her tiny brows. She'd known what my answer would be before she even asked. That didn't stop the little sweet sneak from trying any chance she got though.

Bowie sprang into action. "I'm sorry, ladies. What can I do for you today?"

"We've come for tea," I told him.

"Well, you've come to the right place then. And the best table in the house just happens to be available." He grabbed a couple of menus before guiding us towards the empty table by the window. "Ladies, if I may?"

He proceeded to pull out both Sage and Olive's chairs for them. Just as I reached for my own chair, he folded his hand over mine. "I got this," he told me. My shoulder brushed his hands as I took my seat. I straightened in my seat, breaking our contact. The last thing I needed was for him to feel my suddenly sweaty back. I did, however, sense him lean in a little closer and say soft enough for only me to hear, "Good to see you again, Nora."

Great. Now my panties were soaked, too.

"Now, please tell me, what kinds of tea do you like?" How he flipped from growly ginger to sweet and hospitable shop owner in the blink of an eye was beyond me.

"Cake!" Sage shouted. At the same time, Olive answered, "I don't like tea."

"Okay." Bowie smiled. Judging by his easy demeanor, I ventured a guess that this wasn't his first-time serving children. That only added to his hotness. "Well, the good news is there's a tea for everyone, even people who don't like tea. Though, I'm telling you right now, I'm going to try to change your mind about that. And for you my dear," he said, addressing Sage, "every pot of tea comes with a plate of scones, mini-sandwiches, and biscuits – what you call 'cookies'."

The way his lips formed around the foreign (at least to him) word made me chuckle. His attention turned to me again. "And while this may be a British tearoom, it is a British tearoom in Los Angeles, so you might be keen to know that all our sweets are gluten-free. We also offer alternative milk options."

"That's alright," I told him. "They prefer their milk straight from the cow. But thank you for telling us. Great idea, by the way." His lips turned up with pride. And why not? He should be proud of his business.

"Might I be so bold as to make a recommendation?" Great. Not only did he have an accent, but he was polite and proper, too? My Mr. Darcy kink had officially been engaged.

"Please," I answered.

"Seeing as the holiday season is upon us, I recommend giving our Sleigh Bells tea a go. It's a caffeine-free, herbal blend of jolly fruits, candied orange, and a hint of cinnamon spice." The tea sounded delicious. However, Bowie could've described last week's garbage and I probably still would've thought it sounded scrumptious. "If you want to do the traditional high tea, that comes with a two-tiered tray of gingerbread cake with lemon glaze, sugar plum scones with clotted cream and jam, and Ziggy Stardust's tea sandwiches."

"Ziggy Stardust?" I asked.

He smirked. "Why do you think my mums named me Bowie?"

"Cute." I couldn't tell if it was the man or the menu that had my mouth salivating. "What do we think, girls?"

They both nodded, Sage more enthusiastically than Olive, but that was to be expected. "I'll get right on that," he said. "Let me know if you need anything else." Bowie gathered our menus before flicking his gaze to mine. "Anything at all."

I couldn't help but feel like he was offering a lot more than scones.

Bowie

I will not wank off in my place of business. I will not wank off in my place of business.

The phrase had circled round my mind like a record on repeat for going on an hour, ever since Nora had entered my shop. I'd just about combusted when she'd insinuated that I'd been a naughty boy this year. What I wouldn't give to get naughty with Nora.

This train of thought is doing nothing to curb my hard-on.

Truth was, I had a healthy appetite for all kinds of sex – some naughty, some not – with people of all genders. So long as everybody was a consenting adult and on the same page with their desires (and boundaries), I was on board. There wasn't much I wasn't willing to try or try again. Except for fire play which had quite literally, scarred me. I didn't even keep candles in my apartment anymore.

But that was all private knowledge. I didn't publicize the goings on inside my bedroom to anybody except my best bloke, Killian. And he was 5,000 miles away.

My "employee", Leighton, was a close second. I used the term loosely, because she was pretty much the closest thing to family I had on this side of the pond. Much to her chagrin, I'd quickly wormed my way into her "cold, dead" heart – her words, not mine. Like me, she'd had her heart broken ten too many times. That's what happened when you wore your heart on your sleeve, and Leighton and I were two sleeves cut from the same cloth.

"You going to ask her out?" My surly work-sibling in question asked, causing the piping bag to slip from my hand. Apparently, I'd been too caught up in my lust to hear her enter the kitchen.

"Who?"

"Don't play dumb, you little shit." Only Leighton could make "little shit" feel like a term of endearment. "I'm going to take a wild guess and say that's the same pink-haired vixen you met at Thanksgiving."

"Violet." I spoke without thinking.

"Her name's Violet?"

"No," I told her. "Her name's Nora. But her hair, it's not pink. It's more...violet. Like fields of lavender or–"

I looked over my shoulder to find Leighton leaning against the counter, utterly enthralled. "Oh please, go on," she said around a smile. "Like fields of lavender or?"

I grumbled and turned back to the cookie I was frosting. "Those her kids?" Leighton asked.

"No, she's their nanny," I told her.

Over the course of their visit, I'd come to find out Nora nannied for Sage and Olive. Sage, who had to be the happiest little girl I'd ever set sights on. Her joy was infectious, so much so that I'd found myself smiling every time I left their table. Olive, on the other hand… Though I couldn't put my finger on why, Olive reminded me of Nora. They both seemed somewhat guarded, like they kept their cards close to their chest. It made me wonder what cards Nora was holding on to, and which ones she kept closest to her heart.

"So, now that we've clarified her hair color and profession, I repeat. Are you going to ask her out?"

"I don't know. I want to, but…" I sighed.

"But what?" Leighton badgered.

"But I just ended things with Kendall."

"And?"

"And aren't you the one who's always telling me to cool it and 'just be single for once'?" I asked, throwing Leighton's words back in her face. Well, gently tossing them. I hadn't thrown anything at anybody's face since my recreational rugby days back at Uni. The only thing I threw these days was an ass-kicking Oscar party.

"What I said is that you should take a break from *relationships*," she said. "There's a big difference between relationships and casual dating."

"Oh really? And who are you *casually dating* these days?"

She flicked the tea towel she kept tucked in her apron at me, nailing me in the thigh. I knew myself enough to know that I was shite at casual relationships. Flings, one-night stands, hook-ups, whatever you wanted to call them. *Shite.* I loved being somebody's boyfriend and more than that, I was bloody good at it. But maybe it was time to try something new.

So long as I got to try something new with Nora.

Seeing as we'd only spoken a couple times now, and always in the company of other people, I knew I was getting ahead of myself. I delivered the plate of freshly decorated snowflake cookies to Nora's table and watched as Sage's eyes grew three sizes bigger. Even Olive licked her lips.

"On the house, ladies," I told them. "My thanks for being my favorite table of the day."

"You didn't have to do that," Nora said.

"My pleasure. Can I offer anyone another cuppa?"

"You talk funny." Sage giggled.

"Sage," Nora warned. Her admonishing tone triggered something in me. I didn't think I'd mind her using that tone with me. Preferably in bed.

"It's alright." I bent down so I could face the littlest girl head-on. "I know I talk funny. But this is just how we talk in England. In fact, if you're ever to visit, I think you might find they think *you're* the one who 'talks funny'".

She chewed and smiled. I pivoted my body to face Olive. "And what about you, lass? Do you think I 'talk funny'?"

I couldn't be sure, but I thought I saw the telltale sign of a smile. Or an almost-smile, at least. "You talk like Mary Poppins."

"Is that right?" I crooned. According to the friends I'd made in the states, my accent had always been a wee bit dodgy. But that's what happened when you grew up on the England-Scotland border. I didn't sound anything like Mary Poppins, but Olive didn't know that. "Practically perfect in every way?"

"Wow, somebody knows his Mary Poppins," Nora teased.

"Well, you know what they say…" I pushed the jar of sugar cubes across the table towards Nora. "A spoonful of sugar helps the medicine go down."

And I kid you not, there in front of the children, Leighton, and the dancing Santa I had tucked in the corner, she picked up a sugar cube and tucked it directly into her mouth. I just about came in my trousers as I pictured her tongue flicking the cube, side to side inside her mouth. Her lips kicked up. She knew exactly what she was doing, and that more than answered my question. Nora was feeling me as much as I was her.

"Look Nora, Bowie's fingers match mine."

Sage pointed to my fingernails, which I'd just painted a deep velvet blue last night. Unlike my namesake, I'd never fancied fashion or make-up. Instead, I'd gravitated towards colorful nails at an early age. Some people might have an issue with it, but that was their issue, not mine. Sage's hand looked tiny next to mine, almost doll-like. But she did in fact have a similar shade of blue on her nails.

"Well, look at that," I marveled.

"So, he does." Nora nodded. "And what do we think of that?"

Sage looked from her hand to mine and then back at hers once more. "Beautiful in blue!" she shouted.

I shifted my focus to Nora. "Beautiful in blue, pretty in pink," she explained. "Stunning in silver..."

"Gorgeous in green?" I suggested.

"Magical in magenta!" Sage added.

"Yummy in yellow." Surprisingly, that one came courtesy of Olive.

"As you can see, we're a big fan of painted nails around here," Nora said, gesturing to her and her charges. "They make everything so much more..."

"Merry and bright?" I asked cheekily. She smiled. This was it. This was the perfect moment to offer her my number. "Um listen. I was hoping that maybe you and I–"

"Nora, I don't feel so good," Sage announced. The effervescent child who'd delighted me all afternoon had suddenly paled. I silently cursed myself for bringing out that extra plate of sugar cookies. Without a moment of hesitation, Nora jumped to her feet, quickly paid the tab, and ushered the girls towards the door, all within a matter of minutes.

Seeing as Sage had climbed into Nora's arms, leaving Olive with not one, but two backpacks to carry, I held the front door open for all three of them. Just as I began to close the door behind them, Nora turned back and mouthed a silent, "Sorry." And with that, they were gone.

"Nicely done, Mary Poppins," Leighton murmured.

"Fuck off." I knew it was just the two of us. We were an hour away from closing and only one party had come and gone since Nora and the girls had sat down. "I was just about to give her my number." I started clearing away the empty dishes from Nora's table. "And Mary Poppins? She's the one that's the nanny. If anything, I'm Bert."

"Please. You've got nothing on Bert."

"Bert's got nothing on me."

As we cleared the dishes together, I couldn't help but wonder if I'd missed my shot with Nora. Twice now, we'd come and gone like passing ships in the night. If those ships were anthropomorphized and wanted to fuck each other. Maybe it just wasn't meant to be?

Then again, contrary to popular belief, Los Angeles was an awfully small town. One where everybody knew somebody, and somebody might just be your ex-girlfriend's sister's roommate. I could always ask Riley for Nora's number, though there was something inherently tacky about asking your ex's sister for her roommate's number. No, I think this one was better left up to the ficklest of bitches, fate. Well, fate and perhaps a dash of Facebook stalking?

Chapter Three

December 3rd

Nora

"How dare you accuse me of murdering my own brother!" I cried before spinning away from the detective in a melodramatic huff. Not too quickly though. The last thing I wanted to do was jostle the oversized hat off my head.

"Don't you mean your... *lover*?"

The audience gasped.

Being an actor in Los Angeles had its ups and downs and one of the biggest downs was seasonal work. Thankfully, I had my nannying gig year-round to subsidize the cost of classes, workshops, etc. in addition to the basics like rent and health insurance. I'd booked two commercials this year and had also landed a semi-regular modeling gig for a mid- and plus-size fashion brand, so money wasn't as tight as years past. However, many performers relied on the gig economy for supplemental income these days, and my gig was dinner theater.

"That's quite the accusation, Detective Frost." I laughed haughtily over the sound of clattering silverware. My character, heiress June Jingle III, was only one of the many people suspected of murdering international toy-dealer, Kristoff Kringle. Spoiler alert, she didn't do it. In fact, little did the audience know that I'd be dead before dessert. "Do you have any proof?"

"Just a forged birth certificate and a gut feeling." Yishan, the actor playing Detective Frost tonight, was by far my favorite of the people who played him. He always hammed it up and unlike Kurt, who played Frost on Friday nights, he didn't mouth my lines to me. As if I didn't know them.

"A gut feeling?" I spat. The cheesy lines left a bitter taste in my mouth, but the audience seemed to love it. "If that's all, Detective, I've got a holiday party to get to. Why don't you come and see me as soon as you have something more than your... belly full of jelly." I threw my scarf over my shoulder with a flourish and stormed off the stage.

This was my second year performing in *Murder on the Ornament Express* and as far as holiday gigs went, it sure beat the hell out of retail. Or playing Mrs. Claus for the Queen Mary's Christmas festival. Or serving Christmas canapés and snowy-blowy scallops at the Hollywood elite's holiday parties. Or...

"June Jingle, I presume?"

Of all the murder mystery dinner theaters in all the San Fernando Valley, he had to walk into mine. *The nerve.*

I spun to face the Brit who'd been haunting my fantasies as of late. The same Brit I'd masturbated to two nights in a row. I'd just about worn my favorite vibrator raw thinking about riding that freckled face.

Feigning my best calm demeanor so as not to give away just how much this man affected me, I said, "June Jingle, *the third*, if you must know." I flirtatiously raised my brows, though in hindsight, I must've looked ridiculous. A gaudy, oversized hat (something you might expect to see at the Kentucky Derby), a garish dress decorated in tinsel (with a scarf to match), and face full of stage make-up that up close, made me look like a Vaudevillian clown.

"My mistake." He smiled. Neither of us spoke after that. We did take the time to study each other. And I took my time committing every detail to memory, from his tousled ginger locks to the thin-rimmed glasses he wore, which together, made him look like Ed Sheeran and John Lennon's love child. That would all make for one interesting fantasy later tonight, I'm sure.

"Are you–" I started.

"Oh, how's–" he said at the same time.

We both let out a laugh, before he tried again. "I just wanted to ask how Sage was. I feel terrible for cocking-up her first high tea."

"No, no, not at all." I reassured him. "They both had an amazing time. *We* had an amazing time," I amended. And we had. No tummy ache could mess that up. What did mess me up was the way Bowie said the word, "cock". I'd be thinking about that for a while. "She's fine. Back to her usual, chaotic self."

"That's good." When I didn't say anything more, he lifted his brows. "Weren't you going to ask..."

"Right!" *Stop thinking about his cock, Nora.* "I was just going to ask... if you're following me. Three times in less than two weeks seems like more than a coincidence."

He tucked his hands into his pockets and rocked forward, which immediately drew my attention to his crotch. *Annndd I'm thinking about his cock again.* He might've been a short king – made even shorter by the character heels I was wearing today – but judging by the outline of his cock, he had the big dick to match his energy. Those khaki pants left little to the imagination.

"Would you be flattered or creeped-out if I said I knew you worked here?" he asked nervously.

"I'm not quite sure," I told him.

Had he been some random dude from Tinder, I'd be reaching for my pepper spray – if I was wearing my normal street clothes, that is. And if bingeing the My Worst Date Podcast had taught me anything, it was that "nice guys" usually still expected something in return from their dates. They were just less obvious about their assholery and misogyny. I didn't get either of those from Bowie, though.

"Tell me more."

He sighed. "I saw on your Facebook that you work here. And by happenstance, the owner's also been into Althea's a time or two. I rang her up, asked which nights you were performing, and..."

"Sandy just told you?"

"Not at all." He rubbed the back of his neck with one hand. "In fact, you should be proud to have such a protective boss."

I smiled. That sounded more like Sandy, the sixty-something grandmother of ten who'd made a career playing "the final girl" roles in 80's slasher movies, before using the money to fund the dinner theater. "And yet you're here."

"Well, I may have offered to donate a weekend's worth of desserts to the show. Cranberry Framboise Custards and Sticky Figgy Pudding. In exchange for some... information, of course." I had to hand it to him. His persistence was somehow endearing.

"So, you bribed her."

"Hey, you call it bribery. I call it..." he fumbled.

"Bribery?" I supplied.

He shrugged. "I just um, I never got the chance to give you this the other day." He held out a folded piece of paper. It didn't take long for me to realize that he'd given me his number. "And look, after this, I promise I will stay away. How do you say it? 'The ball is in your court now.'"

Damn this man for making me want to break my own rules.

I bit my lip, probably wreaking havoc on my lipstick, and turned my head towards the stage. *Oh shit.*

I spun back to Bowie. "One second," I told him.

I tiptoed to the edge of the curtain and listened carefully. It didn't matter how hot I found this guy or how... natural our chemistry was. I was a professional. I wasn't going to miss a cue for him. For anybody. Thankfully, Yishan was still mid-monologue which meant I had another thirty seconds or so before I needed to be on stage.

I dashed back to Bowie. "I have to go on in a second but thank you. I'm glad you came by."

"So, not creeped-out then?"

I took the piece of paper with his number and folded it over again before tucking it into my ample cleavage. All without breaking our eye contact. I had to give the guy credit, too. His gaze didn't slip further south at any point.

"Not at all," I told him before turning back to the stage. June Jingle III still had to die tonight, but after that, I had a date with my vibrator and some of Bowie's Sticky Figgy Pudding. *Gulp.*

Sticky indeed.

Bowie

"She'll call, you daft prick," Killian said over the phone, his words washed in humor. Killian might've been my best mate, but he was also my oldest one. We'd met during primary school, when both of our families had signed us up for after school football. Even at seven,

Killian had dominated the field. I, on the other hand, had found solace on the sidelines. Picking grass.

For Killian, it'd been the start of a very successful, athletic career. He'd gone on to play at Uni and eventually, climbed the ranks to a professional footballing career with Leeds United. A decade-long career that unfortunately, had ended prematurely after a knee injury sustained in a car accident last year. His football days were over and that was something he was still grappling with. I was constantly encouraging him to visit California – if for nothing else, then to just get away – but so far, all my attempts had been unsuccessful. We still had a standing call though for every Saturday night, or Sunday morning for him.

"You can't know that for sure," I told him. I felt a tug at my ankle. "Banger, get off!"

"Aw, how is my favorite naughty sausage?"

Banger, my short-haired, miniature Dachshund, continued tugging at my pant leg. I'd say 90% of the time, she was a well-behaved, well-mannered dog. The other 10% though? Uninhibited terror. Apparently, by committing to creating a weekend's worth of desserts for *Murder on the Ornament Express* – and ultimately, trying to win Nora over – I'd pissed off my dog.

Romantic partners came and went, including Spencer, the ex I'd co-adopted Banger with, but Banger was forever. She was used to being the center of attention. That was my fault, really. When Spencer and I broke up, I assumed he'd want to… share custody of our dog. Instead, he'd moved to Austin with his new boyfriend, and I'd showered Banger with extra attention to make up for it. God forbid I ever become a parent. I'd spoil any child rotten.

"Your favorite naughty sausage is just that. A naughty sausage." I scooped Banger up from the floor and dropped her down beside me.

She immediately nestled into my armpit and draped her head across my chest. Between the busy day at Althea's – we'd been fully-booked every weekend for going on three months now – and the visit to the theatre, I was exhausted. My thirty-one-year-old body just couldn't handle twelve-hour days like it had five years ago. Here I was, laying in bed at 11 p.m. on a Saturday night. "You could always come out and see her sometime. I'm sure Banger would love that."

"Maybe." He sighed.

I didn't push him. We'd been best friends long enough for me to understand when he needed space.

"Don't change the subject though," Killian said. "Correct me if I'm wrong, but didn't you just end a relationship?"

"I mean, not 'just'. We called it off a month ago..."

"What happened to staying single for a while?" he asked. For somebody who was so different from Leighton, they sure shared a lot of the same opinions.

"I am. I just thought we could, I don't know... hook-up."

There was a slight pause on the other end of the phone before, "Hook-up?"

"Yeah, you know. Date casually."

"Casual? You?"

"Piss off." I said, loud enough to alert Banger who raised her head off my chest. I pet her smooth hair until she laid back down. "I'm trying. I can't help who I fall for or when it happens."

"I disagree," Killian harrumphed. Our athletic abilities weren't the only things that separated us. While I was a die-hard romantic, Killian was a commitment-phobic bachelor through and through.

"Doesn't matter anyway," I told him. "It's up to her now. She has my number, so we'll see what happens next."

"What happens next is she calls, you date, you fall in love too quickly, she runs." Normally, I was a fan of Killian's brutal honesty. As far as I was concerned, everybody needed at least one friend who would tell you what you *needed* to hear, whether you wanted to hear it or not. Between Killian and Leighton, I got that in spades, though Killian's advice was usually shaded a bit more pessimistically.

"You jealous, Kill?" I asked, eager for a subject change. "You know I'll never love anybody as much as you."

Even through the phone, I could sense his smile.

"Twat." A one-word response that in Killian-speak, may as well have been the equivalent of "I love you, too." I'd take it.

We talked for another ten minutes before ending the call. It was nearing midnight in Los Angeles, but the day had just begun in Leeds. I rid myself of my clothes, changed into a fresh pair of boxer briefs, and performed my usual pre-bed routine before tucking myself into bed beside Banger. I'd given up on crating her through the night after the little escape-artist had somehow squeezed out of her crate (again) and promptly destroyed every shoe I owned while I slept. She looked cute but deep down, she was a possessive, vengeful bitch. God, how I loved her.

I'd just plugged my phone into charge for the night when my phone chirped, alerting me that a text message was waiting. A text message that sent my cock from the semi-hard state it'd been in since Thanksgiving to a full-blown salute.

The message from an unknown number was brief: *Ziggy Stardust called. He wants his name back.* Another text followed almost immediately after: *BTW it's Nora.*

Crisis averted. She'd texted. I typed out my response: *The name is Poppins. Mary Poppins.*

She replied almost instantly with the wind, umbrella, and spoon emojis. Damn, why was that so much more alluring than an eggplant or peach? I'd never been attracted to somebody's emoji game before.

Three dots popped up on screen, which let me know she was still typing. And then–

(Nora) *So, I was wondering how you felt about beer?*

(Me) *Well, I'm British, so... favorably.*

(Nora) *And how about ugly Christmas sweaters? Er, I guess 'jumpers' for you British folk.*

She signed that one with a winky face. Cheeky lass.

(Me) *I may have a holiday jumper (or two) knit by Althea, herself.*

(Nora) *An Althea original?! I'll have to see it to believe it...*

(Me) *Just tell me when and where.*

(Nora) *How about next Saturday at the SANTA Monica Pub Crawl? Starts at 3.*

It'd been years since my pub-crawling days, so I didn't know if I could quite literally, stomach that much alcohol. However, if it meant an afternoon with Nora...

(Me) *Count me in.*

(Nora) *Awesome! Ok, off to bed. Sweet dreams MP.*

(Me) *MP?*

(Nora) *Mary Poppins. Keep up, Bo! Night.*

She punctuated her last text with an "*x*" and a kissing emoji. So much for the sleep I desperately needed.

I slid my hand under the sheets, down my torso until I reached the band of my briefs. It didn't take much to nudge the cotton aside and wrap a firm hand around my cock. I groaned loudly. There was no reason to suppress the sound. I lived alone – apart from Banger, who was already soundly sleeping on her side of the bed – and the walls were thick.

I spread the pre-cum already leaking from the tip down my thick length. Fuck, that felt good. As I stroked my hand up and down, I pictured Nora. I pictured her removing one of her cropped shirts – the ones that hung so well off her full breasts and teased the tattooed curves underneath. I pictured her spreading her legs to give me an unencumbered view of her gorgeous, wet pussy. I pictured her slipping her fingers in and out of her pussy and rubbing her clit with the same vigor as I was currently rubbing my cock. My cock twitched at the thought of a front-row seat to her self-pleasure. Would she like that? Me watching while she fucked herself to climax. *I know I would.*

I sped up my strokes and used my other hand to cup my balls. My fantasy took shape. This time, Nora climbed up my body and slid herself slowly down my cock, until every delicious inch was surrounded by her warm, wet heat. I'd let her set the pace at first, let her take her time riding me and grinding her clit against my body. Whatever she needed to climb that peak. There wasn't anything sexier than a partner who knew exactly what they needed to come... except maybe, being the person to help get them there.

I'd be happy to lend Nora a... helping hand.

As soon as she'd reach that edge, I'd roll her over and take her from behind. I wouldn't have to go slow. I wouldn't have to worry about leaving a mark if I gripped her hips too hard. No, Nora's thick, rounded body was ready for a rough fuck. My balls tightened, orgasm just out of reach. I was practically lifting my hips to meet my hand with each thrust. It wouldn't take much more to send me over the edge.

I pictured myself winding a hand around Nora's body and reaching down to finger her clit, all while she screamed around a mouthful of sheets. *Fuck that, I want to hear her screams.* That's all it took to send me over the edge. The thought of hearing her and feeling her, of feeling myself pumping deep in and out of her, made me erupt. I moaned as a stream of cum shot across my bare chest. It took a minute to finally catch my breath and another few to clean up in the loo, but after that, I had no trouble falling asleep.

And I did so with a smile on my face.

Chapter Four

December 10th

Nora

"**I** don't think I've ever seen so many Santa's in one place before."

Bowie was right about that. The "SANTA Monica Pub Crawl" certainly lived up to its name. There were Santa's left and right. Slim Santa's. Thick Santa's. Blue-haired Santa's. Booty-short Santa's.

While Bowie and I had dressed for the occasion – him in an "Althea original" hand-crocheted vest, me in an atrociously decorated sweater I'd thrown together a few years back for an Ugly Sweater Party – we were two of the only people in Barney's Beanery not decked-out in Santa garb. Barney's marked the third stop on our pub crawl around the Santa Monica promenade and my calves (and liver) were starting to feel it.

We'd began our afternoon with some Rudolph shots at Cabo Cantina, which I'd venture were strong enough to turn anybody's nose red. I was also thanking my lucky stars that we'd taken the time to enjoy some chips and salsa while we were there. My stomach had been in knots all week about an audition I'd had for a TV pilot. Auditions were a dime-a-dozen and rejection was just part of the industry, but damn, I really wanted this part. If for no other reason than to prove that fat girls could play leading ladies, too. According to my agent, Ali, I'd be hearing about it any day now.

That compounded with the typical first-date butterflies had really thrown my eating habits the last few days. I was trying my best not to think about it and the sickly-strong drinks we'd imbibed over the past hour or so had helped.

Bowie's company helped, too. Aside from my roommates, I couldn't remember the last time I'd had so much fun with somebody.

"I guess we should've taken the name more seriously," I said.

"Oh well, next time I guess."

"Are you saying that you've got something more... Santa-ish at home?" I asked. I can't say I'd ever had a thing for Santa, but a ginger-haired, bespectacled Santa with a British accent? I could get on board with that.

"Maybe."

He smiled and sipped his Adios Motherfucker. Scratch that... his (*Yippie Ki-Yay*) *Adios Motherfucker*, a drink name designed to piss off anybody who refused to believe that "Die Hard" was a Christmas movie. The cocktails at Dudes' Brewing Company, our second stop of the afternoon, had been strong but they were nothing compared to Beanery's selection. I'd always had a high tolerance for alcohol, but I was in my mid-thirties now. Melatonin gummies knocked my ass out these days.

"That's okay. I like your 'Althea original'." I gently plucked at a loose thread dangling from the shoulder of his vest, half-expecting the entire thing to unravel. The vest had clearly been crafted with love, not skill. But the mish-mosh of reds, greens, and gold juxtaposed brilliantly with Bowie's pale complexion. "Speaking of Althea, you never mentioned how Althea's Tearoom came to be."

"That's all Nan, Althea herself." He rubbed his chin. "She moved to the States years ago. Something about getting away from the British 'gloom and doom.'"

Over the course of the past week, Bowie and I had texted constantly. One thing I'd learned was that he adored his family. He'd always found a way to weave his moms or best friend, Killian into almost every conversation we'd had. And not in a creepy, overly dependent *"You'll never measure up to my family"* kind of way. I'd encountered that plenty in my two decades worth of dating in Los Angeles. No, Bowie *loved* his family. Like "love them because you want to, not because they're your family and you have to" kind of way. Even a stranger could take one look at the way Bowie's eyes twinkled when he spoke about his grandmother and know exactly how much she meant to him.

Holiday fling, Nora. Holiday fling.

I'd been repeating the mantra for days, desperately trying to remind myself that I wasn't looking for a relationship. And just when I'd have myself convinced, he'd text me again, the chirp of my phone unleashing a swarm of butterflies in my belly.

"She was lucky to snag the property when she did, and at a bargain price no less," he continued. "It helped that she'd tucked away a good bit of money when my granddad passed..."

He trailed off, but I knew he wasn't finished. My eyes fell to his lap where he was currently using his drink-free hand to trace invisible circles. I slid my hand to cover his. His eyes met mine and silently, I let him know to take the time he needed.

"I moved to LA about five years ago and started working with Nan shortly after. She died a year later."

"I'm sorry to hear that."

"Thank you," he told me. "She was the one who first introduced me to baking. And we did a *lot* of baking together this time of year. Seems like no matter what I do, my gingersnaps never have as good a crunch as hers did."

He smiled sadly.

We sat like that, surrounded by a bar full of Santa's, his hand in mine, for several minutes. At some point, he rolled his hand over to interlock our fingers. He'd painted his nails red and green since I'd seen him last. I couldn't help but think about how our hands rested perilously close to his denim-covered bulge. *Don't ruin the moment by thinking about his dick, Nora.*

"Why did you move?" I asked him.

"To LA?" I nodded. "I, uh... followed a girlfriend."

Well, that was enough to kill *my* boner. Not my buzz though. I removed my hand from his and took another sip of my green-colored drink. "What happened there?"

He rubbed the back of his neck. I'd seen him do it enough times to recognize the tell. He was embarrassed. "You really want to talk about exes on the first date?"

Definitely not. *Way to bring up the number one faux pas of dating*, I mentally scolded myself. "If I say no, does that mean there'll be a second date?" I asked him. I wasn't above flirting shamelessly, especially if it meant getting Bowie into my bed.

From the way his eyes lit up, I could tell we both had the same thing on our mind. I was seconds away from making a move when my cell phone buzzed across the bar top. My agent's name filled the screen, immediately sending my stomach plummeting to the booze-soaked floor. "Sorry, do you mind if I take this?"

"Of course not."

"I'm sorry. I normally turn my phone off on dates, but it's about that audition and–"

He cut me off. "Nora, you have nothing to apologize for. Go take the call and I'll grab us another round."

Geez, why did his words make me want to cry? That'd be something to explore during my next therapy session.

I navigated my way through the sea of tipsy Santa's and towards the door to the outdoor patio. As soon as I made it far enough away from the blaring music, I answered Ali's call.

And how I wish I hadn't.

***

"'Too big and too bubbly,'" I slurred. "That's what they said. Can you believe that?"

I sucked what was left of my North Pole Negroni through the straw, drawing out every drop until there was nothing but air.

"Bloody daft, if you ask me," Bowie said. He took the empty glass from my hands and set out of reach on the bar.

Hands now free, I reached for his arms. I'd always been a bit of a touchy-feely drunk, emphasis on the "touchy". And it was safe to say that after drinks five, six, and seven, all in a matter of minutes, I'd officially reached Carrie Bradshaw-level "drunkity drunk drunk". When my hands met Bowie's biceps, I was surprised to find them so pronounced. Considering his smaller frame, I hadn't expected them to be as thick or... hard.

"Thank you."

Whoops, apparently drunk me had said that last bit aloud.

"I don't get it," I told him, giving his arms a squeeze.

"Well, I lift weights a few days a week and I row on the weekends." He smirked. *Smartass.*

"Noooo," I drew out. "The part. It called for and I quote, a 'take-charge woman whose personality is almost as big as her hips.'"

"They really said that?" He furrowed his brows.

"Yeah, Hollywood is nothing if not direct. Especially when it comes to what you look like."

"There'll be other parts, yeah?"

"Of course." I belched. *How ladylike.* "Excuse me. I'm used to rejection. Every actor's used to rejection. And plus-size actors face a lot more rejection that straight-size folks."

"What was special about this part?"

I thought about it. Even in my drunken stupor, I had trouble coming up with an answer. "Honestly, nothing. This part wasn't anything extraordinary. I guess I'm just tired."

"Of acting?" he asked.

"No!" I protested. "I love acting. I can't imagine doing anything else. I guess I'm tired of always coming in second. With jobs, relationships... I just want to be somebody's *first pick* for once. That probably sounds selfish though, huh?"

"Not at all," he told me.

The rejection call from Ali had been short and anything but sweet. It didn't take long for Bowie to recognize the hurt, or the fact that I was trying to soothe it by quite literally drowning my sorrows. After a second drink at Barney's, we'd headed over to Brittania for Ginger(bread) Beers, and I'd decided to try to single-handedly drink my weight in Mistletoe shots.

I'd lost count around six.

It wasn't like me to get completely fucked-up like this, especially when I was with somebody I barely knew, in a bar on the complete opposite side of town... Come to think of it, I didn't even know what bar we were in at this point.

"Hey, where are we?" I gave his arm another squeeze.

"Ye Olde King's Head."

I snorted. "Sounds very British."

He laughed before wrapping his hands around mine and dragging them from his arms. "Trust me, it's not." He stood and hands still in mine, pulled me up, too. I was suddenly thankful I'd decided to wear flats tonight. Had I worn the heels I'd originally picked out, I'd most likely be on my ass by now.

Crawling out of the pub. During the pub crawl.

"I think it's time we call it a night."

I didn't have the energy to resist, so I just let him guide me out of the bar. I let him order us a Lyft back to my apartment and despite what I'm sure was a hefty charge, he didn't say anything about it. I let him use my phone to text Riley and let her know we were on our way back. I even let him hold my hand as we waited for the car to arrive.

I found purchase leaning against the side of the yoga studio next door, away from the noise inside the bar. Bowie stood in front of me, protecting me from any wayward onlookers without crowding me against the brick wall. Talk about being effortlessly sexy.

I want this man.

I'd always gone after what I wanted. I'd gone after my acting career even when my parents had pressured me to pursue something "more stable" instead. I'd gone after practicing yoga despite the amount of people who'd told me that it wasn't for "big girls" (or the side glances I *still* received in class each week). And hells-bells, I'd gone after every man that had interested me over the years. I wasn't about to stop now.

"Hey," I said softly. He looked up from his phone, where he'd been keeping an eye on our Lyft driver's status. I leaned off the wall and knotted my hand in that hideous – but cute – sweater of his and dragged him towards me. He could've stopped me, and knowing what I already knew about Bowie, I'm sure he would've if I was asking for more than a kiss. We both knew that our car would be here any minute. There wasn't time for more than a kiss.

Instead, he let me take the lead, and pull his body closer until the tips of my breasts brushed his crochet-covered chest. Rather than touch me the way we both wanted him to, he placed his hands beside my head, caging me in against the bricks. A warm, woodsy blend of cinnamon and pine suddenly bombarded my senses, a combination of this evening's cocktails and Bowie's natural scent. What I wouldn't give to take a bath in that smell.

For a second, maybe two, maybe thirty, we stood there. His gorgeous green eyes locked on mine, his delicate pink, lips slightly parted. Just enough for him to inhale every exhale of my breath.

And then just like that, he slammed his mouth to mine. The kiss was unexpected, to say the least. Not the act itself, but the fervor with which Bowie kissed. There was nothing sweet or soft about this kiss. No, this kiss was an invasion. A duel, really, because I was giving it back to Bowie just as zealously as he was me.

He broke our kiss to suck in a breath. "Fuck, Nora," he growled, before diving back in.

I tugged on my fistful of his sweater, attempting to pull him further into me. This time, our tongues tangled. I felt him hardening against my thigh. And all the while he kept his hands pinned to the wall beside my head. That is until he lowered one of his hands to my throat.

I don't know what surprised me more; the fact that this sweet, cinnamon roll of a man who wore sweater vests knitted by his grandmother and said things like, *"Cheerio"* to passing strangers, had his hand wrapped around my throat. Or the fact that I liked it.

Scratch that. I fucking loved it.

He held me there to the wall, hand gripping my neck, thumb resting against my pulse point to gauge my response. It wasn't rough. I didn't feel uncomfortable in any way, save for the brick wall digging into my back. In fact, I'd venture that I'd never felt safer with a man, at least not one I'd only been on one date with. There was something both comforting and terrifying about that realization.

I could've stood there kissing Bowie for hours. Unfortunately, our Lyft arrived a few minutes later, rudely bringing a sudden halt to the tongue-fucking of the century.

Bowie

It'd been a while since I'd held somebody's hair back while they vomited in the bushes. And yet, here I was, hands tangled in Nora's lilac locks, failing miserably to focus on anything else but the sound of her retching.

When we'd piled into our Lyft, I'd been fully prepared to take her home, cuddle for a while until we both sobered up, and then pick things up from where we'd left them outside the bar. We'd spent the bulk of our ride back to her townhouse in silence, her head resting on my shoulder. The moment we'd gotten out of the Lyft however, she'd lurched for the plants. I hadn't realized that she'd crossed the line from drunk and flirty to drunk and about-to-be violently ill. Otherwise, I might not have kissed her.

And damn, it'd been one hell of a kiss.

I couldn't lie. I'd envisioned a set-up much like this over the course of the last week. Nora, kneeling before me, my hands tangled in her hair. But this wasn't quite what I'd had in mind.

"I'm so sorry, Bowie," she moaned. "I ruined our date, didn't I?"

I squatted beside her, keeping a careful hold on her hair. "You joking? This isn't even the worst date I've had this year." I swiped a bead of sweat from her brow.

She smiled weakly. "I don't know if I believe that, but even if it's true, you can go. You don't have to stay for this."

I ignored her. "Do you think you're ready to get up?"

"Yeah." She moaned again.

"Slowly," I warned when her knees buckled. I wrapped an arm around her side and urged her to lean into me. She did so grudgingly, grumbling all the while. I had a hunch that Nora Sanders wasn't one to willingly lean on anybody, physically or metaphorically. I'd take what I could get.

I led her towards the skinny, two-story house, past the small, well-manicured yard dotted with succulents and other desert plants. That's about all the greenery the Los Angeles climate allowed for. Vegetables didn't fare much better, either. When I first moved into Gran's cottage, I'd planted some tomatoes and cucumbers. Most of them had died within months thanks to LA's tropical heat. The fucking squirrels had taken care of the rest. *Demon buggers.*

Before I could rifle through Nora's handbag for her keys, the front door opened. Riley leaned against the frame.

"Well, I'll be." She folded her arms across her flannel pajama set. "Is that a Nora under all that alcohol?"

Nora mustered up enough strength to flip off her roommate. "Is that my roommate under all that asshole?"

Riley's laugh subsided as soon as she noticed Nora's pale face.

"C'mon honey bunny. Let's get you in the shower." She pushed off the door frame and wrapped an arm around Nora's other side. I slowly (and reluctantly) let her go. "Bowie, nice to see you again."

"Same here."

She added, "Dev's in the kitchen crafting their magical hangover elixir, if you want to help."

"No, he doesn't have to stay," Nora protested, even as Riley guided her towards the stairs. She looked back at me over her shoulder. "You don't have to stay."

"Don't worry about me." I winked at her.

I wiped my feet on Riley & Devin's "You're here, we're queer. Get used to it," doormat before crossing the threshold and shutting the door behind me. Glancing around the open concept living-dining area, it wasn't hard to pick up pieces of Nora scattered amongst the otherwise neutral space. A purple, animal-printed pillow on the L-shaped couch. A photo of Nora, Riley, and Devin framed in glittery gold. A highlighted script amongst the stack of history papers Riley had clearly been grading on the dining room table.

I'd met Riley and Devin a few times while dating Kendall and though they each had their own flare, neither of them were nearly as... expressive as Nora. Riley never had a hair out of place. For goodness' sake, she wore matching pajama sets. In fact, Riley's compulsive organizational skills and need for "perfection" were traits that Kendall had often complained about. Devin, on the other hand...

If what they said about opposites attracting was true, Riley had certainly met her match. By all accounts, Riley and her spouse were polar opposites. Whereas Riley had grown up in suburban Southern California, Devin had been raised on a "communal-living" farm in rural Vermont. Riley preferred the stability of her high school history teaching position. Devin, on the other hand, worked as a freelance glass artist, creating everything from art pieces to elaborate pipes (which may as well have been art pieces).

After a few minutes, the upstairs shower kicked on. Rather than muse about the likelihood that Nora was probably naked right about now, suds sluicing down her curvy body, I continued my perusal of the house.

I found Devin in the kitchen, preparing what I assumed was their so-called "magical hangover elixir" in the blender. Like Riley, they were already dressed for bed, too. Only Devin's bed clothes – well-worn sweatpants, a faded band tee, and a sleep bonnet used to cover their box braids – looked a lot more like what I wore to bed. Apart from the bonnet, of course.

"Hey," I greeted.

"Hey. Didn't think we'd be seeing you so soon again."

I smiled. It was hard to believe it'd been less than two weeks since the Millers' explosive Thanksgiving. "Oh, congratulations by the way. I don't think we ever really got a chance to celebrate your marriage."

Devin snorted. "That was kind of the point of eloping. To avoid any kind of big celebration." They added a few more things to the blender – some Gatorade, a slice or two of ginger, and... was that a splash of tequila? I lifted my brows. "Hair of the dog," they explained. "Besides, Ri's mom is insisting we have an actual ceremony, so if you're available December 26th..."

"Wow, so soon?"

"She wants to do it before Kendall jets off to Thailand or Indonesia or wherever." Devin rolled their eyes before starting the blender. They raised their voice to speak over the noise. "Seriously though, it's just going to be a small thing in their backyard. You're more than welcome. Especially since you're dating Nora now."

"I'm not... We're not..."

"What?" they shouted, a twinkle of humor in their eyes. They were clearly fishing for information. But how could I share information I didn't even have? I didn't want to presume that there was something more to my relationship with Nora than there was.

It's not a relationship, you wanker.

"I don't know if –" They abruptly turned off the blender. Judging by the sudden quiet echoing through the house, Nora must've shut off the shower sometime during our conversation. I glanced towards the stairs, making sure we were out of earshot, before turning back to Devin. "I don't know if I'd call it dating," I said, this time in a much lower decibel.

"Yeah? What would you call it?" I looked away as Devin poured the positively ghastly looking beverage into a glass. "It's been years since I've dated but chasing after somebody's whereabouts by bribing their employer with desserts seems like something more than 'casual' to me."

I tucked my hands into my pockets. "We're just... having fun."

It wasn't a lie. So, what if I wanted more than that? It didn't matter what I wanted if Nora and I weren't on the same page.

Devin stared, the amused look on their face never wavering. "Fun, sure." Their gaze dipped to my chest. "Nice sweater."

I took the glass from their outstretched hand. "Up the stairs, second door on your right." Before I reached the stairs, they added, "Oh, and Bowie. Spare blankets and pillows are in the closet under the stairs."

I didn't bother correcting them. There was no reason for me to spend the night. Nora was home safe and (mostly) sound. She had her roommates. What did she need me for? Boyfriends stayed the night, not first dates who dry-humped you against brick walls. Decision made. I'd deliver her hangover helper, give her a quick kiss goodbye (on the forehead, of course) and head home.

I knocked lightly on Nora's bedroom door. When she didn't respond right away, I knocked again. Still no answer. I slowly turned the knob and pushed the door inward, inch-by-inch. "Nora?" I whispered.

A part of me assumed she'd already gotten into bed, fallen asleep even. What I hadn't expected though, was to find Nora sitting on her bedroom floor, clad only in a towel. A towel that did positively nothing to hide her luscious dips, folds, and rolls. On the contrary, her body was on full display. In fact...

Fuck, I can see her nipples.

It took all of two seconds for me to realize what a massive invasion of her privacy this was. I spun away from her.

"Bowie?" she asked quietly.

"Um, yeah, it's me. I'm sorry," I told her. "Devin asked me to bring up their... mysterious hangover cure. I knocked, but you didn't answer." She didn't respond and I wasn't about to turn around again, so I just kept talking. "I thought you might've fallen asleep, so I was just going to drop it off and go, but–"

"I'm naked."

Trust me, I know that.

"Right. I didn't see anything, I promise." My body was in desperate need of a subject change. "Do you want me to just leave the drink?"

"I tried to get dressed, but I got dizzy and sat down."

I swallowed. "Do you need some help?"

"I can just call for Riley. You don't have to..."

"No, let me." I scoured the room for a place to set down the disgusting concoction. If I caught one more whiff of it, Nora wouldn't be the only one spewing their guts. I set the drink down on the nearby wardrobe, pausing momentarily to admire the photos and jewelry laid out on top. I turned back to Nora, keeping my focus averted from her body. "Okay, what can I do?"

"My pajamas. They're in the closet. Second bin on the left."

I looked up from the floor to see her pointing towards the door on the other side of the room. *Fuck*. I'd have to walk right by her to get there.

"Okay." I quickly ducked across the room towards the closet. I tried my best not to notice the fresh scent of Nora's body wash or shampoo, and instead focused on the task at hand. I grabbed an old shirt and a pair of boxers before rethinking the latter. If she was having trouble standing up on two feet, there was no way she'd be able to slide her legs into shorts one leg at a time. The shirt would have to do. Besides, it looked like it'd be long enough to cover her body.

Shirt now in hand, I crossed the room back to Nora. There was no way to avoid looking at her now. And what I saw was a very beautiful, very naked woman still seated on the floor. I squatted in front of her, much as I did with Sage and Olive that day at Althea's. Maybe she was embarrassed, maybe she was genuinely concerned about covering her body, but either way she kept her eyes on the floor. I tilted her chin up, bringing her gaze to me.

"Shirt first, then bed," I told her. It wasn't a question, but she nodded anyway. "I'm going to hold out the shirt and close my eyes. You let me know when everything is covered." She nodded again.

I bunched the fabric together and held it out front of me, facing Nora. And just as she let go of her grip on the towel, I shut my eyes. I used every ounce of willpower I had to keep them closed. Even when I heard the towel drop to the floor. Even when I felt her lean forward so she could pull the shirt down over her body.

"Okay, I'm covered." I waited another second or two before opening first my right eye, and then the left. What a surprise... she was a vision in blue cotton.

Together, we carefully got her up and over to the bed. I pulled back the covers and waited patiently for her to crawl into bed. I pretended not to notice the way her curvy bottom peeked out from beneath the fabric. She pretended not to care. Once she was settled, I still made her take a few sips of Devin's drink before laying her head down. She grimaced after each gulp.

After she'd drunk more than half, she laid down and closed her eyes. She moaned as I stroked her head and rearranged the wet hair that had fallen across her face. It made me wonder what else made Nora moan. Hopefully, there'd be plenty of time to find out.

It wasn't until I felt her breathing even out that I leaned down and lightly pressed my lips to her forehead. I may have sniffed her hair, too, but that was beside the point. All I knew was that suddenly, Devin and Riley's couch didn't sound so bad after all. Plus, I made a mean plate of banana pancakes...

So much for keeping things casual.

Chapter Five

December 11th

Nora

*W*hat kind of monster blasts Mariah Carey at 8 a.m. the Sunday morning after a bar crawl?

I did my best to shield my face from the sunlight streaming in from the bedroom window. It helped that my eyelids were practically welded shut with last night's mascara. Apparently, I'd had the sense to shower in last night's drunken daze, but not enough to remove my make-up. Not my finest example of adulting, but still better than waking up in puke-covered hair, something I hadn't done since my twenty-first birthday.

When Mariah's "All I Want for Christmas is You" segued into N'SYNC's "Merry Christmas, Happy Holidays", I knew there'd be no going back to sleep. What were they listening to? *Now That's What I Call A Very Merry Millennial Christmas*? I sat up, threw the blankets off me, and realized almost-immediately that the bottom half of me was completely unclothed.

Full-on Winnie the Pooh style.

I let out a yawn and was suddenly flooded with memories of the night before. My date with Bowie. The pity party-turned-drinking binge. An incredibly epic (and incredibly public) make-out session. Throwing up in the bushes (something else I hadn't done since my twenty-first birthday). Bowie helping me put on my pajamas. Bowie putting me to bed. *Wow, I really know how to show a guy a good time.*

I'd be sure to text him later to apologize… after I butchered my roommates for blasting their holiday playlist.

After washing my face, I pulled on some joggers and threw my hair into a messy bun. I descended the stairs almost comically slow, using both hands to grip the railing. Just as I reached the final step, the intoxicating aroma of something sweet hit me hard. Devin and Riley would be the first to admit that neither of them had the "baking gene", so I couldn't fathom what they'd be up to in the kitchen this early in the day. Or why it smelled so good.

"Okay, which one of you suddenly learned to cook?" I called out, loud enough for them to hopefully hear of the music.

"It isn't us," Devin said from behind me.

I spun to find them and Riley fresh from sleep, much like me. Sundays were usually the one day a week we'd spend together, lounging on the couch watching movies, cleaning the house, and meal-prepping for the week if we felt extra motivated. It didn't surprise me that they were still in their pajamas. What surprised the hell out of me was the fact that somebody other than me or my roommates was cooking in our kitchen.

My mind raced through the possibilities. *No, it can't be…*

As if conjured straight from one of my favorite fantasies, Bowie entered the dining room just then, carrying a plate of pancakes. He was wearing the same clothes as last night, sans Christmas sweater vest. Even now in my hangover haze, I couldn't help but wonder what he'd look like wearing *only* his sweater vest. Did I have a crochet kink?

No, I have a Bowie kink.

"Oh, great. You're all up." He wiped his hands on the dish towel tucked into the waistband of his pants. "I, um, woke up early. Habit. So, I thought I'd fix you all something for breakfast. Oh!"

Riley, Devin, and I all exchanged a look of disbelief when he rushed back into the kitchen only to return seconds later carrying a bowl of fruit. Fruit that he'd not only cut, but also arranged into a decorative design that you'd expect to find at an upscale Beverly Hills brunch spot, not our NoHo townhouse. "I hope you don't mind that I took advantage of what you had in the pantry."

He pulled out the chair at the head of the table. It took a couple of seconds for me to realize he was offering me the seat and a couple more to close my gaping mouth. I wasn't used to men cooking for me, let alone men I wasn't sleeping with. And he'd cooked for Riley and Devin, too?

The three of us took our seats at the table. While Riley and Devin poured themselves juice, Bowie hand-delivered a mug of coffee to my side. "I wasn't sure how you liked it."

"Black is fine. Thank you." I placed my hand over his and lowered my voice. "You didn't have to do all this. If anything, I should be cooking *you* breakfast. Although, I'm not much of a chef, so I'm not how much of an apology that would be, but–"

"You have nothing to apologize for." He rolled my hand over in his and stroked his finger across my palm.

With anybody else, I might've doubted the words coming out of their mouth. Hollywood was, in a word, transactional. I was used to people saying what they needed to say to get something out of me and honestly, I'd be lying if I said I hadn't done the same. But somehow, I knew Bowie meant what he said. There was no malice or hidden meaning behind his words. Only understanding.

We spent the next hour enjoying breakfast and to nobody's surprise, it was amazing. The banana chocolate-chip pancakes were exactly what my body needed to soak up the last of the previous night's alcohol. Bowie, Devin, and Riley did their best to ease my guilt by trading drunken horror stories. As it turned out, Bowie had his fair share of "shame receipts" to share, one of which included waking up on a sheep farm in Wales. Ever the history buff, Riley asked him all kinds of questions about U.K. destinations and monuments. And he promised Devin he'd have his moms send them some sea glass after their next trip to the shore.

At one point, Riley leaned over to whisper, "Marry him." I'd retaliated by hurling a strawberry slice at her and she'd promptly fussed about me staining her favorite pajama top.

After polishing off the last of the pancakes, we all discussed our plans for the day. "Well, seeing as we're getting married–" Riley began.

"Again," Devin finished, perfectly in-sync.

Riley smiled. "Mom is insisting that we get engagement photos taken."

"Even though you're already married?" Bowie asked. My body was hyperaware of the fact that he'd rested his palm on my upper thigh, right on top of my tattoo. It'd taken all of ten minutes for me to pick up on the fact that Bowie enjoyed physical touch. Throughout breakfast, he'd found any excuse to touch me. A hand on my lower back, a brush of his fingers across my neck, and now his entire hand on my thigh. I'd never felt so relaxed and simultaneously, turned on all at once.

"She feels, and I quote, 'cheated out of planning a wedding'. Since Kendall isn't getting married any time soon…" Riley's eyes widened after she said it. "Sorry."

"Don't worry about it." Bowie smiled and sipped his tea. As it turned out, he was a tea drinker through and through. If five years living in Los Angeles hadn't made him an artisanal coffee drinker, nothing ever would.

"I guess she's got her sights set on us," Riley told him. "It's fine. It'll be small and intimate. Just my parents, sister, a couple of cousins who live close by and Devin's brother."

"My mom is currently Eat-Pray-Loving her way around Europe," Devin explained.

"Join the club," I told them. "My mom and stepdad are taking a cruise to Mexico for Christmas. My dad and his girlfriend are spending the holidays with *her* children and grandchildren in Arizona."

Was I somewhat annoyed that I'd be spending yet another holiday with my roommates rather than my own family? Sure. Then again, missing Christmas with them also meant avoiding their passive aggressive remarks about my acting "hobby" and not-so-subtle inquiries about my relationship status. That was the gift that kept on giving.

"What about you, Bowie?" Devin asked. "You going home for the holidays?"

"I wish," he sighed. "I can usually only afford to go home once a year and even then, it's far too expensive in December. We usually end up celebrating Christmas in January or February."

His hand stroked up and down my leg, inching closer to the heat between thighs. I might've put on pants this morning, but I wasn't wearing any underwear. If he moved his hand any higher, he'd know exactly what kind of effect he was having on my body.

"Bachelorette Party!" I blurted. I'd meant it more as a distraction for myself, but everybody was staring at me now.

"Um, what?" Riley asked.

"We should have a Bachelorette Party. Er, Bachelor-X Party?" I turned to Devin and scrunched my brows. Perhaps they had a better idea of the proper terminology.

"Bachelor-X Party. I like that." They turned to Riley.

"Me, too." Riley dropped a kiss on Devin's nose.

Ugh, they were so cute, it made me sick. I'd known Riley for my entire adult life, so naturally I'd been privy to her relationships over the years. Despite all their differences, nobody made Riley as happy as Devin. In fact, she'd told me about two months into their relationship that Devin was "the one", a huge statement for someone who'd spent the second half of her twenties dating a married couple.

When I'd asked Riley what set Devin apart from the rest of her relationships, she hadn't hesitated in telling me that Devin made her "sparkle". At the time, I'd laughed. It sounded so... naïve and child-like. Something I'd expect to hear from Sage or Olive, not a grown ass woman. But watching them now, witnessing the love that radiated between them, I knew exactly what Riley had meant. Even if I hadn't experienced it for myself yet.

"...so, we should probably get going." Riley said. *Oops.* I'd completely spaced-out mid-conversation.

"Sorry, what?"

"Our engagement shoot," she repeated for me. "Dev and I are driving down to Long Beach, and we need to be there by two, so we should really get going. We won't be back 'til late tonight."

"Oh, great," I told them. I guess I'd have the house to myself to veg. Then again, I'd originally budgeted for some holiday shopping today. That had of course been pre-hangover, but still, Christmas was coming up quickly.

"What are your plans?" Bowie asked me.

"Well, I need to do some holiday shopping, but I don't know…"

"That sounds like fun. Do you mind if I tag along?"

The sound of choking permeated the room. I turned to find Riley sputtering her coffee. "You good?" I asked.

"Yup!" She wheezed a couple more times. "That sounds like fun. You guys should do that. Go shopping."

"Well, I…"

"If you'd prefer to go on your own, I completely understand," Bowie said. "Leighton's running the shop today and really, I wouldn't mind some help picking out gifts for some friends and family. I'm *shite* when it comes to gift giving."

Somehow, I didn't believe that.

"Okay, let's do it," I announced. I don't know who was more shocked; me or Riley, who was still having trouble swallowing her coffee. Devin simply shook their head and smiled. They were used to our antics. Bowie on the other hand…

His hand tightened possessively around my thigh which let me know *exactly* how he felt about it.

Bowie

"What's wrong with a bracelet?" I asked.

Nora stepped away from the mustard jumpsuit she'd been eyeing and made her way over to me. I held up the beaded wrap bracelet I'd picked out as a Hanukkah gift for Leighton. "You wanted my advice, remember?"

I nodded. I hadn't been lying when I'd told Nora that I sucked at gift giving. Truly, I loved giving gifts. It was picking them out that I had trouble with.

For Nora, gift giving was a science of sorts. She weighed the pros and cons of every present. Was it big enough? Was it something they'd actually use? Would she be able to safely ship it? Me, on the other hand, I shopped from the heart. Who cared if it was too big or too frivolous or too breakable? I'd figure that out later. So long as it made them happy, and the gift came from the heart. And my heart was telling me that Leighton wanted, nay *needed* this bracelet.

"My advice is that unless she's shopping with you, you should never buy somebody else jewelry."

My eyes widened. "Never?"

"Never."

"Do you really think so little of my taste?"

She cocked a hip and smiled. "Not at all. I just know how fickle I am about the jewelry I wear. Riley's the same way."

"Okay, but..."

"How many exes have you bought jewelry for?"

After a moment of silent counting, I told her, "A few girlfriends." I scratched the overgrown scruff on my chin before adding, "A few boyfriends, too."

"Fair enough," she mused. It might not have seemed like much, but this bisexual boy appreciated her refreshing candor. "And how many of those partners regularly wore the jewelry you bought them?"

I looked at her and then at the bracelet. "Fair enough," I said, echoing her sentiment. I placed the bracelet back on the display and picked up my shopping bags. Together, we exited the store and headed back into the sunshine.

We'd spent the past couple of hours moseying up and down York Blvd. in Highland Park, popping into shop after shop. I'd found a throw blanket and some pottery from a local artisan for my moms. Nora had talked me out of about a dozen more bits and bobbles, reminding me about the time and cost it would take to ship things back home. Instead, we'd scoured Etsy and picked out a few things from U.K. sellers that guaranteed delivery to my moms and Killian before Boxing Day.

Nora had found a planter for her sister at a small vintage shop. Instead of clay or glass, it had been upcycled from old VHS tapes. We'd picked out some vintage records for her dad, who apparently collected vinyl, a socialite's cookbook for her dad's girlfriend, who Nora referred to as "Mommie Blogger Dearest", and some make-up and nail polish for her dad's girlfriend's kids. I'd helped pick out the colors.

I sucked in a breath of fresh air. "God, I love the weather here."

"Warmer than a British Christmas?"

"Absolutely." The temperatures had dropped in the last couple of weeks, but most days easily reached 18 or 19 degrees. Er, Celsius degrees.

"What do you miss most about Christmas in England?" she asked.

"My family," I answered without hesitation.

"Aside from them. Any places to go or favorite traditions or..."

"Well," I started, "we usually spend Christmas at home, simple and cozy. I still make my mums' fruitcake every year."

She scrunched her nose. "Ew, fruitcake. Why?"

"It's not like your *American* fruitcake," I said, in my best Southern Californian accent. "Valley girl," I think they called it. "I'll show you," I added. "No, I think the one thing I miss most are Christmas markets.

There's a great one in Edinburgh I used to visit every year. Mulled wine, Christmas lights, open-air shopping. There's nothing quite like it."

As we waited to cross the other end of York, I traded my bags from one hand to the other and reached for Nora. Not her hand, but rather the small of her back, something I'd noticed she'd enjoyed before. She audibly gulped which made me smile. I liked that I made her a little bit nervous.

Now she knows how I feel.

"Did you want to pop in anywhere else?" I asked her, while using my hand at her back to guide her across the street.

"No, I think I'm done for the day," she said. "I'm still pretty exhausted from yesterday and honestly, I'm starting to lose momentum."

"I'm sorry."

"It's okay." She smiled. "Nothing a nap or some lazy couch time can't fix." When we stopped at the next stoplight, she turned to face me fully. "Trust me, I needed this fresh air."

I thought about leaning in to kiss her but reconsidered. After all, she'd just told me she was practically dead on her feet and even without that, I didn't know how Nora felt about PDA. This wasn't the darkened side of a yoga studio. We were in broad daylight, surrounded by holiday shoppers.

"Er, I know you drove, but I can catch a Lyft home if you prefer?"

"Where do you live?" she asked.

"Monterey Park."

"Monterey Park?! And you hauled your cookies all the way to the beach for some girl?"

I scoffed. My moms were both Broadway buffs, so I hadn't missed the "Grease" reference.

"No, I hauled my cookies all the way to the beach for you."

When I'd moved in with Nan, I hadn't realized just how spread out the city of Los Angeles was. Only in LA could you drive an hour and go no more than a few miles. But Nan had left me the cottage and the price of the mortgage sure beat rent prices in LA, so I'd stayed. The commute to Los Feliz wasn't bad, but generally I didn't spend much time west of Highway 101. And yet, I'd made an exception for Nora. Twice.

"I have a better idea," she said, leaning into me. Just a few more inches and we'd be chest to chest. "Why don't you come over and hang around with me?"

"Yeah?" I asked eagerly, not playing it cool in the least.

"Only if you're okay with a lazy, do-nothing, lay around in pajamas kind of evening. And just so you know, that means Hallmark Christmas movies and greasy Chinese takeout."

I chuckled. "Sounds good to me."

It took us a few minutes to walk back to her car and then pile our purchases into the back. Just as I opened the passenger door, she asked, "Bowie?"

"Yeah?"

"There's going to be cuddling, too."

This time, I was the one who swallowed. "Like I said. Sounds good to me."

***

Nora was a world-class cuddler.

Seriously, if they awarded medals for top-notch cuddling champions, Nora would take the gold. We'd spent the better part of the afternoon wrapped up in each other's arms on her living room couch.

We'd laid side-by-side, legs tangled together, and hands interlocked. We'd laid with her head in my lap, while I played with her hair and willed my body not to respond to how good she smelled. At one point, she'd even had her arms wrapped around me from behind, "big spoon" style. I loved that she was so comfortable with me. She didn't shy away from touching my body, and she let me do the same.

Dinner had arrived midway through our first movie, some ridiculous holiday romance about rival toy shop owners. We'd eaten our Chow Mein and Broccoli Beef on the couch, all the while playfully mocking the film. We'd finished dinner about an hour ago and had since moved on to the second movie. Nora was currently sprawled across the full length of the couch, her legs resting on my lap.

At first, I was grateful for the pair of sweatpants she'd lent me to change into. There was nothing comfy about laying around in slacks. But after a few hours of cuddling, I'd realized the sweats did little to nothing to conceal my hard-on. The hard-on that was firmly pressed against Nora's exposed thigh. Just as I'd swapped my trousers for sweatpants, she'd traded her jeans and sweater for a t-shirt and a pair of loose boxers.

And how did I know her boxers were loose? Great question. Because every time she rolled over or got up to refill her water, every time she adjusted her legs in any way, I caught a glimpse of her knickers. They were blue, they were small, and they were teasing the fuck out of me.

"Okay, clearly, this guy is Santa."

"Sorry?" I asked.

"Are you even watching the movie?"

I laughed guiltily. "No." She'd caught me. How was I supposed to pay attention to a bloody movie when I could practically feel the heat emanating from Nora's cunt?

She nudged my chest with her sock-covered toes. "Why not?"

"Why not what?" I teased.

"Why aren't you watching?"

"Because."

"Because why?" From the way she smiled, I could tell she knew I was being deliberately daft.

"Because I was too busy thinking." I stroked the tattoo, a floral design that climbed her upper thigh, beyond the hem of her boxer shorts.

"Thinking about what?"

I released the breath I'd been holding and met her gaze without a flicker of humor this time. "How I'd like to put my hands in your pants."

She froze but didn't shy away from my penetrating gaze. I didn't move or say a thing. What happened next hinged entirely on her response.

"So, why don't you?"

That was all the confirmation I needed to snake my hand beneath her cotton shorts. It didn't take long to reach her panties, which I was pleased to find were already wet. I ran my fingers over the outside of her panties, once, twice, and a third time, before breaching the fabric with my fingers. I kept my eyes on Nora's face the entire time, cataloging the way her lips parted when she moaned.

"Damn, you're soaked," I told her. I slid my middle finger inside until I was knuckle-deep. Her wet heat practically sucked me in. I peppered her waist with kisses, while my thumb toyed with her clit. The only thing preventing me from getting deeper was the restrictive band of her panties.

I pulled my hand out of her shorts entirely and she groaned her disappointment. She didn't have to wait long though. I dropped her legs to the couch and moved quickly. With both hands, I gripped the waist of her shorts and panties.

I looked up at her and asked, "Is this okay?"

She nodded before slightly lifting her hips, allowing me to tug both her shorts and panties over her ass until she was completely bare from the waist down. This time I was the one groaning.

"Fuck, you're gorgeous." I almost didn't recognize the deep timbre of my voice. Her legs fell open on the couch, making a space for me between them. I slid both of my hands up her thighs until they framed her pussy. I teased the outer lips with my thumbs until she thrust her hips forwards, her patience running thin.

"Bowie, I want..." She gasped when one of my thumbs circled her clit.

"I know what you want, Nora." I leaned forward and laid a kiss on her hip bone. "Now lay back and relax." I punctuated each word with more kisses, slowly moving my way closer to her mound. "And let me give you what you *need*." This time, I lightly nipped her skin, just above her pubic bone. Not deep, just enough to make her lower body lurch off the couch cushion.

And with that, I ate Nora's pussy. Not licked, *ate*.

There'd be plenty of time for gentle licks and sweet caresses later, if I had my way. For now, I feasted on her cunt like she was my first meal in days. My tongue tore through the layers of her pussy, before drawing a line up to her clit. When I circled the small bud and sucked, her legs instinctively tried to trap my head in place. I forced them wide and then draped them over my shoulders. And all the while, my eyes never strayed from hers. I memorized every twist of Nora's hips, every moan, every move that lifted her higher and closer towards release. I used them as my road map. Destination: Nora's orgasm.

"Oh, God," she cried, one hand moving to my hair. She used the other to grip the pillow behind her, anchoring her pussy closer to my mouth. "Bowie, please. Please don't stop."

I had no intention of stopping. Not until she was screaming my name and drenching the couch cushion. My fingers teased her opening while I continued my onslaught of her clit. Her whole body shook as I curled first two then three fingers inside her.

"*Fuucckk*," she drew out in a moan. Her fingers dug further into my scalp, letting me know she was close.

"Come for me, Nora," I all but growled into her pussy. I circled her clit once more. This time, I grazed the swollen bud with my teeth and that was all it took to send her flying. Her body shook as she called out my name before collapsing back on the couch.

I took my time removing my fingers, now drenched in Nora's juices. I reveled in the way her body vibrated yet again as she watched me lick them clean. She swallowed nervously. "I don't have any condoms, otherwise..." She trailed off, blushing.

"That's not what this was about." I told her before lifting myself up her body to take her lips. It was the first time we'd kissed tonight. The first time we'd kissed while sober. And I wasn't about to rush it. I explored her mouth with mine, letting her taste her essence which still coated my tongue. *I wish I could bottle that flavor and hoard it all for myself.* I took my time, coaxing her tongue out to meet mine. I had to leave soon, and I wanted to make sure she'd be tasting me, tasting us, long after I was gone.

When I eventually ended the kiss, I added, "Besides, I've got a probably pissed-off wiener dog just waiting to be walked and fed."

I'd arranged for my neighbor to take Banger before yesterday's date with Nora. What I hadn't planned for was a 24-hour sleepover and cuddle fest. I didn't think my neighbor would mind, but Banger certainly would. "I'm working tomorrow, but are you free on Tuesday?"

Nora bit her lip, hesitating. *Uh oh.* "Bowie, I..."

The sound of the front door unlocking sent us both jumping to our feet. Nora scrambled to grab boxer shorts and panties, while I tried to adjust by rock-hard dick. Who was I kidding? I was still wearing the sweatpants she'd given me, which did absolutely nothing to conceal my hard-on.

Whatever she'd been about to say would have to wait. And frankly, I had a feeling that whatever it was, it wouldn't be good.

Chapter Six

December 14th

Nora

My phone chirped. Again.

"Are you serious?" Riley asked. "You're still ignoring him?"

"Nora, push me higher!" Sage cried.

I tore my focus from my best friend who was currently nursing a gingerbread latte on the playground bench to the little hellion I was pushing on the swings. I'd picked the girls up at school about an hour ago and since their private "academy" didn't have a playground – something about channeling their energy into "productive learning" rather than play – I'd driven them over to the park near our house. Riley had met us with holiday drinks – a gingerbread latte for her, a peppermint mocha for me, and S'mores hot chocolates for Sage and Olive. Just one of the many reasons why I loved her... she kept me caffeinated.

"Any higher and you'll go over the bar," I shouted over the raucous screams and laughter. The playground was packed full of parents and nannies who'd had the same idea I had.

"That's what I want!"

"You won't go over the bar, Sage." Olive never failed to dampen the mood. When we'd arrived at the park, she'd promptly unpacked her bag and begun to do a crossword puzzle. For fun. She'd even brought her Children's Dictionary. "That's impossible. Because of physics."

Where does she come up with this stuff?

"Aren't you a little young for Physics, Ollie?" I asked. When she stuck her tongue out in response, I did the same. It was good to know there was a typical eight-year-old in there somewhere.

Riley leaned over Olive's shoulder and pointed at her puzzle. "Flair. Nine down. Five-letter word for 'style'. It's flair."

Olive's brows furrowed. "Quit helping me."

"Yeah, quit helping her," I echoed sarcastically.

"And *you*." Riley pointed at me. "You quit changing the subject. How many times has he texted today?"

"I don't know," I lied. "Maybe six." Another lie. It was fourteen.

"And how about yesterday? And the day before that?" she pestered. No wonder she taught high schoolers. She'd scare the pants off elementary students. Unless of course, those elementary students were crossword puzzling, tea-hating weirdos.

"What does it matter?" I asked. The truth was Bowie had been blowing my phone up with calls and texts since our night together. Er, weekend together, I suppose. At first, I'd texted back vague responses.

> (Bowie) *I had a great time with you yesterday. We should get together again soon.*

(Me) *Yeah, sounds good.*

(Bowie) *I watched another Hallmark movie last night. And guess what? The guy turned out to be Santa. Again. LOL*

(Me) *Haha. Nice.*

Then, I'd just stop responding altogether. I knew it was a dick move. And it's not that I didn't want to see him or talk to him again. Of course, I did. It wasn't every day you met a sweet and sexy business owner who'd hold your hair back one minute and make you come like crazy the next. I bet he even owned more than one set of towels...

"Four letter word for 'cold feet'?" Olive asked.

"I thought I wasn't allowed to help you." Riley taunted.

"Whatever," Olive grumbled. "Four letter word for 'cold feet'?"

"Fear," I told her.

"Nora," Riley said at the same time. I rolled my eyes and pushed Sage even higher.

"I'm not *afraid*," I emphasized. "I'm just... realistic"

"Oh, please."

"Seriously, what's the point? I'm not looking for a relationship and he shouldn't be looking for one."

I had no doubt that Bowie would make one hell of a boyfriend, but he'd also just gotten out of a relationship. While I was okay being someone's one-night rebound, what I was not okay with was some-body using me to fill a void. I wasn't anybody's placeholder. "This was just supposed to be a holiday fling, nothing more. Somebody to cuddle up to during 'cuffing season'".

"So, cuddle up to him then. You've still got like, two months of cuffing to go."

"Who do you want to handcuff, Nora?" Sage asked. Riley's interro-gation had distracted me long enough for Sage to dismount the swing and tunnel between my legs.

"Bowie," Riley told her. Great, that's exactly what I needed. A six-year-old's opinion on my love life.

"I love Bowie!" Sage announced, pumping her fists in the air.

"You met Bowie once," I reminded her.

"Bowie paints his nails pretty colors. Merry and bright." This is what I loved most about kids. While they tended to over-simplify everything, they also had a knack for finding the beauty in most things, including people. Even ginger-bearded, bespectacled Brits who served them tea. "Why do you want to handcuff him, Nora? Has he been bad?"

Riley hid a smile behind her coffee cup. "No, sweetie, it's just a... thing people say." I told her. Kids might be a lot smarter than adults gave them credit for, but in no way did I think it'd be appropriate to explain 'cuffing season' to a six-year-old.

"It means she likes him," Riley added, wagging her brows.

"Like, *like* likes him?"

"Uh huh."

Sage giggled. "I like liked Bobby B. earlier this year, but that was before he shared his grapes with Amber, and not me. Now, I like like Bobby G." *Oh, to be six again.* "Does that mean I should cuff him?"

"No!" I said quickly and loudly. Loud enough for Sage to know that we'd crossed from playful to serious. I squatted beside her and took her hands in mine. "No," I said again, this time evening out my voice. "Just forget about everything I said, okay?" She nodded. I led her towards Riley and Olive's bench, swinging her little hand in mine as we went. "Oh, and I think you made the right choice about Bobby B. You don't owe anybody anything. Especially if they can't even share their grapes. Does Bobby G. share his grapes with you?"

"Yup. And I share my seaweed packets with him."

Geez. Six-years-old and she already understood the give-and-take every relationship called for.

I turned to Olive. For somebody who had an opinion about everything, she'd been surprisingly quiet. "And what about you? What do you think of Bowie?"

She shrugged. "He's alright." I lifted my brows and turned to Riley, whose face mirrored mine. She'd spent enough time with the girls to know that that was high praise coming from Olive. "Alright" might as well have been "stupendous", in Olive-speak.

I sighed in defeat. Clearly, I was outnumbered. "What if he doesn't even want to hear from me?" I wouldn't want to hear from somebody who'd been actively avoiding me for days. Especially if that person had all but ridden my face and then left me high and dry.

I'd worn my comfiest corduroy overalls today. Riley reached into the front pouch and pulled out my cell phone. "You won't know unless you call him." She held the phone out to me. I eyed it like a bomb, ready to explode at any second.

"Fine." I begrudgingly took the phone from her. "What am I even supposed to say?"

"Well, you could start by apologizing for freezing him out. Ask him to grab a drink or something." Her eyes lit up. "He could run lines with you for your audition on Friday."

"I can't ask him to do that..."

"Why? Because you know he'll say yes?" She was right. There was no doubt in my mind that he'd say yes if I asked for his help.

"Can't you just run lines with me?"

"Nope. I've got report cards to finish, and conferences start tomorrow. I just needed a quick coffee fix and some fresh air before getting started." She picked up her oversized tote and dumped her empty coffee cup in the nearby garbage can. "And before you ask, Devin is holed up in their studio tonight, so you're shit out of luck."

Sage gasped. "That's a bad word, Riley."

"You're right, Oh Sage one. She's... *beep* out of luck."

"Nice. Much better," I said, dripping with sarcasm.

She smirked. "See you later, monsters."

The girls waved their goodbyes and then, it was just the four of us. Sage, Olive, me... and my suddenly very-heavy cell phone. Since when was I afraid to call a boy? I was a thirty-three-year-old woman. I'd visited over fifty countries. I'd colored my hair since I was fifteen. I'd posed for a diamond ad in nothing but pasties and jewel-encrusted panties. I was a goddamn adult. And yet, there was something about Bowie that made me nervous. He made me want something... more.

Something that I had no issue imitating on stage or screen, but had always eluded me in real life.

It didn't take long to find his contact info. It'd only been a few hours since his last text. As I scrolled through the one-sided conversation, I thought about what I'd told Sage. About not owing anybody anything. *Sage advice.* It was a principle I tried to live by, both professionally and personally. In that moment, I realized I didn't owe Bowie anything. But that didn't mean I didn't want to give it to him – give myself to him – freely. And I think that's what scared me most of all.

I hit the call button.

Bowie

"What do you think I want from you?" I asked.

"Nothing that I have to offer."

I dropped the script into my lap. "Well, that's cryptic," I murmured.

Nora tossed up her hands before reaching for another scone. "Okay, so it's not the best script ever." She dunked the scone in the pot of clotted cream, before stuffing the whole thing in her mouth. *Oh yeah, Nan would've loved her.* "But that doesn't make me want it any less," she said, after she'd swallowed, "Plus, it's kind of a big deal. The director used to be Steven Soderbergh's assistant's assistant."

"His assistant... needed an assistant?"

She shrugged. "Everybody in Hollywood needs an assistant. Even assistants."

I shook my head but didn't make any further commentary. No matter how ludicrous I thought she sounded.

After nearly three days of radio silence, to say I'd been surprised by Nora's call this afternoon would be an understatement. I'd pretty much just chalked our entire "situationship" (a term I'd learned from Leighton) to an orgasm-induced fever dream. Her orgasm, that is, not mine. Unless you counted the last three nights of wanking off to memories of Nora's pussy. All that to say, I hadn't expected to hear from her again.

But then she'd called me. She'd apologized for ignoring my texts and chalked her silence up to "being busy". I had a hunch that there was more to it, but the last thing I wanted to do was push her away. If seeing her again meant helping her run lines for her big audition, I was up for the task. Even if it meant slowing things down between us. That didn't matter. She'd called *me*.

"More tea?" I offered, lifting the pot.

"Please." I topped off her cup. "Look, I know that some of the lines are cheesy, but this is my job. It's important to me."

My lips lifted. If there was one thing I admired most about Nora it was her work ethic. Between her nannying responsibilities and acting opportunities, she always seemed to throw her everything into her work. "You're right. I'm sorry."

"It's okay. Let's just take it from the same spot."

I nodded and glanced around the shop. We'd closed early today to prepare for a private party this evening – an elegant bridal shower. I'd already prepped all the food for the event, and Leighton and Hillary, a college student I'd hired part-time, were currently setting the tables. There wasn't much left to do, and thankfully, there wasn't anybody around to witness my awful acting skills (or lack thereof).

I ran a hand through my hair and adjusted my glasses. No wonder I worked in food service. The pressure of preparing for an audition – even though it wasn't mine – was too much for me to handle. I rolled up the sleeves of my jumper to my elbows and turned to Nora. "Ready?"

Her lips were parted, eyes glued to my forearms. "What?"

I smiled. It was good to know that I still affected her in some way.

I leaned across the table and used two of my fingers to gently tilt her chin up. Her gaze met mine. "Are you ready to run it again? I promise I'll behave this time." I winked.

Her cheeks reddened. "Right." She brushed the crumbs from her dungarees and lifted the script to her chest. She took a few deep breaths and then, just like that, Nora wasn't Nora anymore. I'd never dated an actress before, but I had to believe that not every performer escaped so seamlessly into the characters they portrayed.

I waited until she nodded again, before starting from the top of the scene. "What do you think I want from you?"

"Nothing that I have to offer." She was cold and direct.

"April, please. This can't be it."

"What do you want me to say, Charlie? We had our time together and it was great. But..." I hung in wait for her to continue. "But..." She prompted again, looking up from the script in front of her. *Bollocks.* I'd been so caught up in her performance that I'd forgotten my line.

I cleared my throat. "But what?"

"But it ran its course. It wouldn't be fair."

"Fair for who?"

"For either of us. Sooner or later, you'd lose interest. Don't deny it. And even if it wasn't you who lost interest, it'd be me. That's..." This time, it was Nora who fumbled the line. "That's what always happens."

This "rehearsal" had suddenly taken an uncomfortable turn. What was that old saying about fiction mirroring reality? In that moment, somebody was holding a mirror up to Nora and me, rather than April and Charlie, our fictional counterparts.

"That's not true. We're destined to be together. Forever."

"Forever is a fairytale, Charlie," she said dramatically. "Besides, the world will end in five days, unless we stop that missile heading straight for Earth." *Well, so much for reality.*

"Scene." It was Nora, the actress, who was speaking now. Not April, the aerospace engineer.

We set our scripts aside and silently sipped our tea. I studied Nora over the rim of my teacup, while she focused intently on the contents of hers. She clearly didn't want to talk about it – about us – but I needed to know that she wouldn't run again. I needed to know that she was just as interested in me as I was in her before I fell for her. Well, before I fell for her more than I already had. I needed some kind of... sign. *For fuck's sake I've been watching too many Hallmark movies.*

"What time is it?"

I blinked, startled by the sudden shift in tone. "5:45."

"Do you need to stick around for the party tonight?"

"No," I told her. "I already did my bit and Leighton's closing. Why?" I cocked my brow. What was she up to?

"Good. I want to take you somewhere." She hopped to her feet.

"Now? But what about the audition?"

"I'm feeling good about it now. Better than before. Besides, I can always rehearse more later."

"But where –"

"Bowie." She inhaled a deep breath and angled her body in my direction before continuing. "I'm gonna let you in on a secret. I kind of suck at saying what I mean when I mean it. Maybe it's because I chose a profession where people literally tell me what to say and do, but yeah. I'm more of an 'actions speak louder than words' kind of girl." She took my hand in hers and linked our fingers together. "I know I messed up before, but this is me trying to show you that I appreciate your patience with me. Is that okay?"

I took careful stock of the way she bit her bottom lip and the hope that flickered through her milky, brown eyes. Something told me this wasn't a gesture Nora made very often. She'd extended her hand to me, but it may as well have been an olive branch. But did I want to take it? The answer was obvious.

You bet your fucking arse I did.

"I'll drive."

With me driving and Nora directing, it only took about fifteen minutes to reach our intended destination. It took another fifteen to park the car. As we approached the park flooded with twinkling lights and a large crowd of people, I finally realized what was going on.

"So, what do you think?" Nora asked, her arm tucked in mine. "Does it live up to what you remember?"

When Nora had directed us to Echo Park, I hadn't known what to expect. As far as I knew, Echo Park didn't have much to offer after dark, except maybe a night hike and a quick and dirty drug deal (or so I heard). What I hadn't expected to find was row after row of local vendors, all there to sell their artisanal goods to holiday shoppers. Everything from hand-crafted jewelry to personalized pet portraits and even DIY gingerbread kits to create your very own gingerbread Hollywood sign.

I turned to Nora. "Why did you bring me here?"

"Holiday shopping. What else?" She gestured towards the booths. "Wow, that's the biggest gingerbread cookie I've ever seen." I dug my heels into the sidewalk when she tried to pull me towards the booth in question. She looked back at me, her face washed in confusion.

"Nora." I took her hands in mine and turned to face her. "Why did you bring me *here*, of all places?"

She looked back at the festivities. She looked anywhere but at me. "I don't know."

I wrapped a hand around the back of her neck and turned her face towards mine. She'd worn tennis shoes today, which placed her only a couple of inches taller than me. She squirmed under my inspection, so I gentled the hand around her neck and used two fingers to stroke her nape. Finally, she looked at me.

"You told me how much you missed Christmas markets, so I just wanted to give you something, you know?" she said. "A little taste of home."

Her eyes flickered with something. Maybe it was apprehension. Maybe it was anticipation. Perhaps it was a little of both. All I knew was that I didn't want to go another second without my arms wrapped around this woman. Without my mouth on hers. So, I kissed her. My hand tightened around her neck. I pulled her body flush against mine. And wouldn't you know it?

She kissed me back.

Chapter Seven

December 16th

Nora

"Thank you for coming in, Nora." The casting director, a bubbly blonde named Kelli, got up from her seat to shake my hand. In my experience, Kelli's who spelled their names with an "i" were not to be trusted. However, from what I'd seen so far, this one wasn't half bad.

"Thank you."

"And just so you know, the casting process is moving quickly with this one, so don't be surprised if you hear from us as early as next week. Though callbacks will be after the holidays."

"Sounds good." I grabbed my purse and jacket. It was finally beginning to look (and feel) a lot like Christmas. So much so that I'd finally broken out my "winter clothing", aka denim jackets and blanket scarves. The fashionable variety that barely provided any warmth.

"Oh, and Nora," she lowered her voice before continuing. "I can't officially say this, but you should definitely expect a call." She winked.

"Wow." I tried to tamper my excitement, because the last thing I wanted was for Kelli with an "i" to think I wasn't a professional. "Okay, well thank you again."

I did my best not to skip out of the room. Thankfully, I made it past security, out of the building, and around the corner before giving into the excitement. I broke out into my feet-stamping, arms-flailing, hair-swishing happy dance. Right there on the corner, in front of a Yogurtland. I didn't care who was watching (or honking). *Hell, let them enjoy the show!* This was for me, and me alone. Once I'd contained my squealing to a minimum, I started the trek back to the train stop.

Though I had a car, and I'd agree that generally, one needed a car to get around Los Angeles, Friday traffic was an absolute monstrosity. It didn't matter if you left an hour earlier or tried waiting it out by going to the gym. "Not today Satan" didn't apply to Friday traffic patterns in Los Angeles. And there was no way I was going to miss this audition. This audition had been *the* audition.

Every actor had a list of "almosts". The director friend-of-a-friend they *almost* met at a dinner party. The indie film they shot in Palm Springs that *almost* got picked up for distribution by a major Hollywood studio. The pilot they *almost* got a role on before that role then went to the producer's daughter. I could fill the Hollywood Bowl with my list of "almosts".

The thing every actor dreamed of having was *the* audition. The one that put you and your name on the map – and I'm not talking about the one they gave away to tourists on Hollywood Blvd. The audition for *Andromeda 8* had been *the* audition for me. Part of me recognized how silly it was to put so much faith in one audition, especially considering the last one had been such a monumental failure. The other part of me knew I'd killed it.

And the best thing about it? The part hadn't even called for a "big and bubbly" or "larger than life" personality, something every actor knew was just Hollywood-coding for the "fat, funny friend". I think I was just as surprised as Ali when they'd called me in for the audition. And judging by Kelli's positive response to my reading, I was feeling confident. Confident enough to do something I'd never done before.

I checked my phone for directions to Monterey Park. *Crap. Looks like I'm taking the bus.* By my estimates, Bowie would be wrapping things up at Althea's right about now. We hadn't made plans to see each other tonight, but I didn't know if I'd have the same rush of adrenaline tomorrow. Or the courage to do what I wanted to do to him, *with* him, then and there. Nope, it was now or never. *Well, never say never...*

My "rehearsal" with Bowie, and our subsequent date at the Echo Park Holiday Market, had unlocked something in me. And the proof was in my performance today.

With my previous partners, I'd always tried to keep them separate from my work. That's not to say I hadn't invited them to shows or asked for their help with filming the occasional self-tape. When I did though, I'd found that more often than not, they didn't fully support my career aspirations. To them, acting was some unrealistic, girlish fantasy, something I'd assumingly give up as soon as I got married and had kids – neither of which were on my bucket list. Even worse, they'd wanted me to make concessions for them – turn down roles, skip an audition, etc. – regardless of how those concessions affected my "job". Their air quotes, not mine.

Bowie, on the other hand, encouraged my dreams. We hadn't seen each other since the holiday market, but we'd texted and talked on the phone every day. Not just every day. For *hours* every day. He asked me about my inspirations, my teachers. He sent me memes from my favorite movies. He offered me advice, but only after asking if I wanted it first. Most importantly, he made it very clear from the get-go that he was interested in "Nora, the actress", *because* of my ambition, not *despite* my ambition. And if that didn't make me fall harder for him...

Double Crap. In the current traffic conditions, it'd take me a while to get there. Almost an hour. That didn't deter me. Nothing could squash the high I was feeling.

I raced the three blocks to the bus stop, making it just in time to catch the 70 heading East. Thankfully, it was still a little early for the daily commuters, so the bus was mostly empty. That'd make it a lot less embarrassing to send the naughty text I'd been scribing in my head. *Naughty might be putting it lightly.* The more that I thought about it, the filthier it got. But that's exactly what I wanted; to get filthy with Bowie Harrison.

I took a seat in the second-to-last row and dropped my bag beside me. I gathered every ounce of the confidence and charisma currently oozing from my body, and typed out a quick, but very specific text to Bowie. I read it over once, twice, and a third time for grammar. Because who said sexting couldn't also be grammatically correct? And then, before I could overthink it, I hit send.

There was no going back now.

It took about fifteen minutes longer than expected to arrive at Bowie's house and that was perhaps the biggest surprise. Bowie lived in a house. Not an apartment or a townhouse, like me, but an adorable, standalone cottage. It reminded me of Miss Honey's house from *Matilda*. The robin's egg exterior and white picket fence mirrored something out of a fairytale. Then again, the fairytale version would probably include a lush rose garden or assortment of talking animal friends, not desert succulents. It didn't matter how you looked at them. There was nothing romantic about cacti. Phallic? Sure. Romantic? Not so much.

I shut the gate behind me and bounced up to the front door. Bowie had mentioned that he'd moved in with his grandmother before her death which had me thinking this must've been her house. I realized that between his house and the tearoom (not to mention his selection of holiday sweaters), he was constantly surrounded by memories of his grandmother. I wondered if that made him... lonely. Especially with the rest of his family thousands of miles away.

Maybe that's why he's such a relationship guy. Maybe he...

The door busted open, cutting off any further introspection. I yelped as a firm, well-manicured hand dragged me inside.

Ooo, black polish with glitter this time.

"Do you know what your text did to me?" He crowded me against the closed door. I appreciated the way he placed a hand behind my head to cushion the blow. No surprise, even the rough, dominant side of Bowie was considerate. He'd probably spank me, choke me, throw me around like a rag doll... and then say thank you. And you wouldn't hear me complaining.

"I take that to mean you're okay with my request." My hands crept down his chest and towards his pants. He grabbed my hands and pressed them to the door beside my head.

"I just about came in my pants," he growled against my neck. "In full view of all my employees. We were in the middle of a staff meeting." I tried to suppress a giggle, but he must've felt my chest vibrating against his. "You think that's funny?" He nipped my neck. I shut up instantly. "That's what I thought."

When he bit me again, this time rough enough that I knew he'd definitely left a mark, I opened my mouth to scold him. He swallowed my words, crashed his lips down on mine hard and fast. I immediately forgot about any tongue-lashing I'd planned on giving him and instead, let him lash the fuck out of my tongue with his. He pressed his hips to mine, practically anchoring me against the door with his thick length.

He still had my hands caged against the door, so I couldn't touch him like I wanted to. Instead, I lifted one leg and wrapped it around his back – at least as much as my jeggings would allow – and dragged him even closer. He moaned against my mouth.

He was the first to pull his head back and when he did, he was breathing just as heavily as I was. "Tell me again."

I knew what he wanted. "I want to suck your dick until you..." He lifted a brow. "Come on my tits," I finished. He grinned as I echoed the words from my earlier text. Words that would forever be burned in my brain. "Is that okay?" I asked, my confidence waning.

I'd never said those words aloud to anybody. I'd never actually let a guy finish on me either. But the moment I'd walked out of today's audition, I'd had this vision of blowing Bowie's world (while blowing him), and giving him something I'd never given anybody before.

"Anything we do is more than okay," he reassured me, before taking my lips again. Where our previous kiss had mimicked a hard fuck, this one was more like morning sex. Passionate and unhurried.

I wriggled out of his grasp and reversed our positions. His eyes lit up when I pushed him against the door. I reached for his sweatpants and, wait a minute... those were *my* sweatpants. The ones I'd lent him during our cuddle session. "I like your pants," I told him.

He shrugged. "They've become my favorites, as of late."

"That's too bad." His brows pinched together. "Because I'll be taking them back now."

I dropped to my knees. In one fell swoop, I pulled the sweatpants to his ankles. His generous length sprang forward. Bowie laughed as he stepped out of them, and his gorgeous, uncut dick bobbed in my face. Just one more thing I loved about European men: the uncircumcised penis.

In my experience, uncut dicks were like stick shift cars. They might be a little intimidating at first, and an automatic was certainly easier to use, but once you learned how to work a stick, it was more fun to drive. *And* you had more control over the *ahem*, vehicle.

I wrapped one hand around his thickness and used the other to pull back the foreskin. He groaned. "Too much?" I asked.

"Just sensitive."

"Tell me what you like."

"Just don't jerk it too fast and it'll be great. Especially when you put your tongue on me." His lips kicked up on one side. "Focus on the head."

I did just that, teasing the head with my tongue. "Yeah, just like that," he praised. When I leaned in to take him fully in my mouth, he put a hand to my shoulder. "Wait."

At first, I was confused. That was until he pulled me back to my feet and his hands went to the bottom of my blouse. He lifted it up and over my head.

"Fuck, Nora. You're beautiful."

I looked down at my bland, flesh-colored bra. When I'd dressed for today's audition, I'd picked something comfortable, not seduction worthy. I hadn't planned on anybody seeing me topless. Judging by the way he was currently cupping my tits through the thin material, Bowie didn't seem to mind.

Together, we reached behind my back to unfasten my bra. I let Bowie slip the straps down my arms until it pooled on the floor beside the rest of our discarded clothing. He then reached behind his back and stripped off his shirt, leaving him completely bare.

Damn.

He'd been hiding some muscle behind those sweaters and t-shirts. For a minute, we just studied each other's bodies. His, lean with hints of definition (especially around the arms), and mine, soft, rounded, and sprinkled with tattoos. Apart from the design on my thigh, I kept most of my tattoos hidden. They were more for me, than anybody else. Plus, a lot of casting directors frowned on them.

Bowie traced his finger along the paper airplane tattoo beneath my breast. From there, he followed the swell of each breast until he reached my nipples. "I just want you to know," he said, using his thumbs to stroke my nipples. They hardened immediately. "I plan on spending a lot more time worshipping these at a later time."

"It's a date," I told him before dragging his hands away from my tits and dropping back to my knees. "But for now, I want to make you come."

And then I did just that.

***

About an hour later, after I'd sucked the living life out of Bowie's dick and he'd licked me to orgasm yet again, we laid tangled up in his bed half-watching "It's a Wonderful Life," half-discussing Riley and Devin's Bachelor-X Party. Between Christmas plans and their upcoming nuptials, we'd decided that tomorrow night was the only time we could hold the event.

Banger was cuddled up between Bowie and me. In my mad rush to make Bowie lose control, I'd completely forgotten he owned a dog. It wasn't until I'd opened the bathroom door, chest covered in Bowie's cum, only to find Banger sitting *in* the sink, that I remembered. How a dachshund managed to scale a countertop was beyond me, but apparently that was normal behavior for Banger, because Bowie hadn't balked.

I'd put my bra back on after our hallway hook-up, but I'd also traded my jeggings for the sweatpants Bowie had stolen from me. He'd put on some boxer briefs, which did next to nothing to hide his still semi-erect dick. I didn't mind though, and he seemed very comfortable cuddling, his dick nestled between my legs.

"A sex toy?" Bowie asked.

"That's right." The look on his face made me giggle. How he could go from *"I'm going to paint your tits with my cum"* Bowie to bashful *"You want me to bring a sex toy to a party"* Bowie was beyond me.

"And it's a holiday party?"

"Have you ever done a White Elephant gift exchange before?" He shook his head. "A Yankee swap?" No, again. "Basically, you bring a gift – $30 maximum – and we all take turns unwrapping them. If you like what somebody else has unwrapped, you can steal their gift."

"And where do the sex toys come in?"

"Riley and Devin thought it'd be fun." I ran a hand through the light sprinkling of hair on his chest. Red, of course. "Sort of a mash up of a Bachelor-X Party and a XXX-Mas Party."

Bowie snorted. The sound vibrated against my palm. "Americans. Whatever happened to a good, old fashioned Secret Santa?" He wrapped a tendril of my hair around his fingers.

"What fun would that be?" I asked him. "Oh, also costumes are encouraged, so you might want to wear something... spicy."

His hand stopped mid-twirl. "Pardon?"

"You know, Triple X-Mas. XXX." I spoke into his chest. "A lot of our friends get pretty into theme parties, so I'm just telling you they might dress up. You don't have to if you don't want to."

"Will you, um, be dressing up?" He asked in a much lower register. I felt his cock jump against my thigh. *Hmm, I guess I have some shopping to do.*

I smiled against his chest. "You'll see."

He went back to stroking my hair after that. We didn't say anything else for a while, just lay there quietly enjoying each other. Eventually, I put the rest of my clothes back on and he walked me to the door. He had to work in the morning, and I'd made plans with Riley to get manicures before the party.

At the door, Bowie wrapped his arms around my lower back. "You never did tell me," he said, his fingertips grazing the skin beneath my sweats. "Why did you text *me* after your audition? Not that I'm complaining."

"Because I wanted to." I kissed the spot below his ear. He must've enjoyed it, because he angled his head to the side to give me better access. "You were the first person I thought of."

He pulled away from my mouth and looked at me. For a second, I thought I might've said something wrong. That is, until he pressed his forehead to mine and murmured the two words guaranteed to make my pussy clench.

"Good girl."

Bowie

My ordinary Friday had quickly spiraled into anything but. All thanks to the blowjob of the century followed by a midnight trip to a sex shop on Hollywood Blvd. Nora's text message this afternoon had thrown me for a loop – one that I planned on replaying in my head over and over – and her blowjob had rocketed me completely out of orbit. I might never come back down again.

"How about this one?" Leighton asked, holding up something purple, ribbed, and far too long for any human vagina I knew. A double-sided dildo, maybe?

Some people might've found it weird that I'd texted my employee on a Friday night, asking for her advice on sex toys. The timing alone screamed "booty call", but Leighton knew better. I'd explained the concept of Riley and Devin's "Bachelor-XXX-Mas" Party to her, skipping over the salacious details of my evening with Nora, and she'd agreed to accompany me to one of Hollywood's "finest" adult establishments. I guess that hadn't surprised me. Leighton shared a shoebox sized apartment with two roommates in Eagle Rock, both of whom she'd met off Craigslist, so she'd take just about any excuse to get away from her place. Even if it meant a late-night trip to Good Vibes Only with her boss.

"It's got to be under $30." I told her. "And perhaps a bit less... intimidating?"

"Gotcha." She put the oversized dildo back on its shelf. "So, you and Nora have been spending a lot of time together."

Was there a question buried in there? "Uh huh."

"And now you're shopping for sex toys for her."

"I told you, it's for the party game. The White, um..."

"White Elephant," she supplied. Where on earth had somebody gotten that name for a party game? "Still, you're shopping for her. *With* her. Going to a holiday party with her." She held up a leather flogger that I was certain was out of the budget.

"No." I told her. "What's your point, Leigh?"

"I'm just saying." She casually fingered a strand of anal beads. "I thought this whole thing with Nora was supposed to be casual. A break from relationships, remember?"

Bollocks. I'd forgotten about that conversation we'd had, weeks ago at this point. As far as I was concerned, my relationship with Nora was anything but "casual". Then again, we hadn't technically discussed it yet.

"It's still casual," I said defensively. "For now."

She didn't look convinced. "Okay, so you'd be cool with me setting you up with somebody else then. You know, on another *casual* date."

"What? Who?" Leighton had never tried setting me up with anybody before.

"My roommate, Ben."

"Ben? I thought you lived with two women."

"Paula moved out last month and Ben moved in. That's LA, baby." We circled around the back end of the shop. Leighton perused the rack of crotchless underwear. "Anyhoo, Ben dropped off my dance bag at the shop the other day and thought you were cute. Asked for your number."

"You didn't give it to him, did you?"

"Of course not." She held up a pair of panties, covered in cheap, yellow feathers. "What do you think of these?"

"They look like Big Bird's knickers."

She snorted. "Big Bird wishes." She traded the yellow pair for a bedazzled blue thong. "So, should I set it up? You and Ben?"

I rubbed the back of my neck and thought about it. On the one hand, I appreciated what Leighton was saying. In fact, Killian had told me something to the same effect when I'd first asked Nora out. I'd been in relationships for most of my adult life. Maybe now was the time to keep things casual and date around. Then again...

"No."

"What?" Leighton asked.

I hadn't realized I'd said it aloud, but it didn't matter anyway. I didn't want anybody else but Nora. "Thank you, but no. I'm not interested."

Leighton sighed. "Another one bites the dust," she murmured. "Well, alright. Let's find you something appropriate for your Christmas sex party."

"It's not..."

"I know, I know." She moseyed over to the vibrators, while I focused on the arrangement of anal toys. I was no stranger to sex toys, in general, but butt plugs were my favorite. Both to wear and to share. One toy in particular caught my eye. I picked it up and admired the silky silicone. *Yeah, this'll do.* Even better was the price. $24.99.

Perfect. That leaves a few extra dollars for lube.

Though I didn't completely understand the gift exchange game, I knew enough to understand that the likelihood of taking home the toy I brought to the party wasn't high. But in that moment, I wasn't choosing a toy for a sexy gift exchange with friends. I was choosing one for Nora. And if I was lucky, one for Nora *and* me.

"Solid choice," Leighton spoke from over my shoulder. "But now the more important question is what are you going to wear to this shindig?"

A Cheshire cat-like grin spread across my face. Little did she know that I already had the perfect outfit picked out.

Chapter Eight

December 17th

Nora

"What in the Lauryn Hill are you wearing?" I failed to hide my amusement when I opened the door. I'd known they made onesie pajamas for adults, but I never would've expected Bowie to own one, nor wear one to a naughty Christmas party. And yet, here he was.

A reindeer. A fine as hell reindeer at that.

Well, that's something I'd never thought I'd say. Even in my head.

"You like it?" A small smile tugged at his lips.

Of course, I did. There wasn't much I didn't like about this man. In fact, in some strange way, that was the most unlikeable thing about him, his lack of flaws. He was so sweet, so attentive, so giving, in and out of the bedroom. In my experience, that always meant they were hiding something. So far though, Bowie wasn't giving off any red flags.

Quite the contrary, his flags were neon green, and I was ready to go go go.

"It's... cute." I toyed with the onesie's zipper, which ran from just below his neck to just above his crotch. *Mm, my favorite section of Bowie.* "Can I ask you something though?"

He nodded and dropped his hands to my waist. Not that there was much to grasp. The rest of our guests hadn't arrived yet and I was still wearing my bathrobe. "What about this is 'naughty'? Don't get me wrong, you look pretty adorable, but it doesn't exactly scream XXX-Mas."

He bit his bottom lip. "I suppose it depends then..."

"Depends on what?"

"On what I'm wearing underneath."

That had me raising my brows for sure. The party hadn't begun yet and my mouth was already drier than Palm Springs. "And what do you have on underneath?"

He gently tugged me closer. I stumbled slightly, and a satisfactory smile spread across his face when I gripped his shoulders to catch myself. Damn this man and the way he threw me off balance, even with slippers on. He brushed his lips against my ear, his warm breath teasing my skin. "Nothing." He nipped my ear, eliciting a small moan from me. *Fuck. How am I going to make it through the party without jumping his bones?*

Seeing as my legs were practically putty thanks to Bowie, he guided us both into the kitchen and back towards the festivities. Devin was putting the finishing touches on their Christmas charcuter-TREE platter while Riley was maniacally curling ribbons for her wrapped White Elephant gift. They both greeted him but didn't stop what they were doing. Guests were slated to arrive in five or so minutes, but five minutes may as well have been forty minutes in "Los Angeles time". Not to be confused with "football time".

As Riley finished wrapping her gift, I suddenly realized that Bowie had arrived empty-handed.

"Did you forget your White Elephant gift?" I asked him.

"No, it's in my car." He drew circles along my back as if it were the most natural thing in the world. As if my body was an extension of his. "I'll grab it in a moment, but I wanted to see if you needed any help first."

"That's sweet," Riley said. She dropped the immaculately wrapped rectangular box on a small pile of gifts under our faux tree. By comparison, my gift looked like it'd been dressed by Sage's Girl Scout troop. "I think we're just about set here. Why don't you go get your gift." She pointed to me next. "And you go finish getting ready."

I took off up the stairs. As excited as I was for the party, I was more excited for Bowie's reaction to the outfit I'd planned for tonight. It only took a few minutes to slip my tightest pair of jeans up and over my ass. My nearly naked ass, thanks to the see-through thong I was wearing. I relished in the way the rough denim rubbed against my pussy lips. I had no doubt, I'd be rubbing my thighs together more than once this evening. Even now, I could feel myself growing wetter by the second. All thanks to a stupid sexy reindeer.

A few minutes later, I spritzed my curls with a touch of hairspray and plumped my breasts up one last time before descending the stairs. I'd heard the doorbell ring a few times, so I wasn't surprised to find a few of our friends crowded around the dining room table, loading up on snacks. My eyes scanned the room, searching for my red-headed Rudolph. I found him in the living room, perusing our bookshelf. Truly, it wasn't fair how good his ass looked in a pajama onesie. I sauntered over to him, as quietly as one could in heeled boots.

"I hope you don't plan on reading all night," I teased.

He turned and proceeded to drop whatever book he'd been considering. "Bloody hell, you look incredible."

I held out my arms and turned, much like a ballerina in a music box. *More like ballerina meets sexy Mrs. Claus.*

He raked his gaze over my body, from the over-the-knee, faux leather boots to the jeans that did wonders for my bulging hips, before finally landing on the semi-see-through corset. It was mostly lace, with boning and strategically designed patches of red silk. All threaded together by two silk ribbons which knotted in a bow at the top of the structure.

"Seen enough?" I asked him.

"Not nearly." A devilish grin stretched across his face.

"Everybody grab a drink!" Riley called from the other room. She was a one-woman party-planning parade. I'd bet money on her having tonight's festivities scheduled down to the second. "It's time for White Elephant."

"Do you hear that?" I turned back to find Bowie inches from my face, his warm, spicy scent surrounding me. "It's time to open some presents."

"And how about this?" He fingered the silk bow between my breasts. One flick of the wrists, and he'd undo the corset entirely. "Do I get to unwrap *this* present later, too?"

I gulped. "We'll see."

***

Two mulled wines, three gingerbread cookies, and one hit of weed from Devin's pipe later, and I was having a great time. Merry and bright, some might say. It was Bowie's turn in the gift exchange game. He'd drawn number ten, and seeing as there were only twelve of us, ten was a fairly decent spot to be in. Everybody knew, however, that when it came to White Elephant, the best was last. And for the first time in I don't know how many years, I'd drawn number twelve. I'd have my choice of everybody's gifts and damn, there were quite a few to choose from.

Devin had picked a pair of fuzzy handcuffs, a tried-and-true bedroom gift for newlyweds. From there, I'd seen our friends unwrap some role-playing dice, a bullet vibrator shaped like a snowman, and some edible candy underwear. Riley had drawn a small flogger, which had promptly been stolen by her teacher friend, June. We'd hung out with June quite a few times over the years and one thing I knew for sure from living with a high school teacher... teachers partied hard. June's partner merely blushed when June straddled our couch, whirled her flogger through the air, and sang her own garbled rendition of Ginuwine's "Pony". And that was all before ten p.m.

My partner in fictional crime, Yishan had just about cried when he unwrapped the most beautiful, glass dildo made to look like a candy cane. Devin's glass work was something to behold, and we all knew something like that would retail for well over $30. I gave everyone a look that said, "All of y'all better not take that from him." So far, it'd worked.

"What'd you get?" Riley bounced in her seat, like a kid on Christmas morning.

Bowie held up his prize. "Nipple clamps." A chorus of "oohs" followed.

When he sat beside me once again, I whispered low enough for only him to hear. "I picked those out."

"Oh really?" He raised his brows. "So, is that something you might be... interested in trying?"

"Definitely." I wetted my lips. "Definitely interested in trying."

I looked down in time to see him cover his lap with the unwrapped box. It was refreshing to see him this way, out-of-control. Even better to know that I was the one who made him feel that way.

"My turn!" Percy shouted. Percy handed the glass pipe, another one of Devin's handmade creations, off to her husband and chose one of the final wrapped gifts. I recognized the wrapping on this one immediately. This was Bowie's gift. "Oh wow," she started, her eyes running wild over whatever she'd just unboxed. She held it up for all of us to see. "It's a butt plug. A vibrating butt plug."

My entire body fluttered. Just when I thought I'd figured this guy out, he went and introduced vibrating anal toys...

I was up next, and I had a big decision to make. But I wasn't about to do it without checking in with him first. When my eyes met his, I recognized the longing in them. It was matched only by a devious glint that had turned his normally hazel eyes a darker shade of green.

I knew he'd never push me to do something, anything that I wasn't comfortable with. Bowie got off on making me feel good. And I knew that tonight, that butt plug would make us both feel good.

So, I stole it from Percy.

Bowie

As soon as we entered my house, I was on Nora. An urgent frenzy of hands, lips, and teeth.

My mouth tore at hers while I pressed her against the front door, leaving no room between us. We'd been here before, but it was different this time. Tonight, there'd be no interruptions from dogs or roommates. When I'd dropped Banger off at Leighton's on the way to the party, I'd given her strict instructions not to call me for the next twenty-four hours, unless there was an emergency.

Tonight was all ours.

I wasted no time in pulling down one of the corset cups to free her hefty breast. All night, I'd been focused on catching a glimpse of Nora's almond-colored nipples. Knowing they were barely contained behind the thin fabric had been torture.

I kissed and licked her skin, before swirling my tongue around her exposed nipple and sucking it into my mouth. I'd never understood why some women were so picky about dating shorter men, because even with Nora in heels, I was the perfect height for ample tit stimulation.

She in turn unzipped the front of my onesie, drawing the zipper all the way down my sternum, past the light feathering of hair, until it stopped just above the root of my cock. She wrapped a hand around the turgid length and pulled it free of the fabric. I moaned against her breast.

Two can play that game.

She jolted off the door when I slid a hand down her front to cup her pussy through her jeans. "I can feel how hot you are." I rubbed a finger along the seam. "How wet you are."

"Bowie, I can't wait any longer."

"What do you want, baby?" That was the first time I'd used any sort of endearment with her, though my intent was anything but endearing. I wanted to fuck this woman into the next millennia, but first, I had to make sure we were on the same page. "Nora, what do you want?"

"I want you to fuck me." She clutched a fistful of my hair and dragged me back up her body. I groaned before taking her lips again in a punishing kiss. With a hand at her back and the other wrapped around her neck, I guided her toward the bedroom.

"I should tell you," I whispered against her lips. "Kendall's the only person I've been with in about six months."

She pulled her head back. "It's been almost a year for me. And I just got tested for STIs. Negatory."

"Mine, too." That had me curious. She hadn't been with anybody in almost a year, but she'd had a recent STI screening? "When'd you get tested?"

"Last week." Her cheeks pinkened. "I didn't want to get my hopes up, but I wanted to be prepared. In case we, you know…"

"In case we fucked?" I lightly nipped the crease where her shoulder met her neck. In response, she turned us until she could push me down on the bed. When she backed away from the bed instead of climbing on top of me, I sat up.

"Stay," she ordered before beginning to strip. I leaned back on my elbows, the sides of my onesie still split open to expose my cock. She started with her boots. While I was sad to see those go, I knew she needed to remove them in order to take off her pants. I made a mental note to fuck her later in those boots (and only those boots). Her denim pants followed shortly, leaving her in nothing but her corset and barely-there, matching thong. When she reached for the bow at the front of her corset, I growled.

"Uh uh, baby. That's *my* present to unwrap."

She stepped between my legs and watched as I slowly unlaced her corset. I didn't miss the way she licked her lips when she noticed the bead of precum leaking from the tip. So long as she was distracted.

As soon as the corset fell to the floor, I dropped to my knees. Nora gasped when I thrust my tongue deep into her pussy. She slid her hands through my hair and tugged my face closer, practically grinding herself against my mouth. I held her delicate thong to the side as I devoured her cunt. Her hips jerked when I slid two fingers inside her, stretching her wide. When I used a third finger to drag her natural lubricant up and around the puckered ring of her ass, before pressing it inside, she detonated. I continued licking her through her orgasm.

As she came down, I hurriedly fitted myself with a condom. Once I had it in place, I pulled her to straddle my cock. She lowered herself in one long stroke, burying my cock in her soft, silken pussy. I'd never been a religious man, but *Jesus fucking Christ,* I could've sworn I saw heaven.

Thankfully, she took her time adjusting to my length. As it was, I was barely holding on to what little composure I had. I'd been waiting for weeks to get inside of Nora. I wasn't about to mess this up by finishing before we even got started.

I tugged her bottom lip between my teeth. "You good?"

"So good," she breathed against me. "God, Bowie. I don't know if I can move."

I wrapped my arms around her, sliding them down to the globes of her ass. With my feet firmly planted on the floor, I lifted her up before slamming her back down onto me. She cried out, her nails digging into the back of my neck. My muscles contracted as I continued to pump in and out of her, and eventually, she took the lead.

She pushed my chest until I laid back completely. She laced my fingers through hers and pressed them to the bed beside my head, using them for leverage as she rode my cock. I laid back and enjoyed the show. The swell of her breasts, the way they bounced each time she sat back on me. The tickling sensation of her thong scraping up and down my cock. At this rate, I'd be lucky to last five minutes.

And then, I had an illuminating thought.

"Hop off, baby." She grumbled. "Just for a second, I promise."

She reluctantly slid off my lap, her pussy leaving a trail of wetness in its wake. I raced to the front room where we'd dropped our coats and bags and retrieved the item I was looking for. Good thing it came pre-charged.

Nora's eyes lit up when I held up the butt plug. "We'll save the nipple clamps for next time," I told her. She nodded. "Nora, I need your words."

She did one better. She rolled onto all fours, putting her ass in the air. She looked up at me over her shoulders. "Do it."

I saw red.

I stripped away my ridiculous reindeer getup, then uncapped the bottle of lube that'd come with the toy and rubbed a generous amount on the bulbous head. I lubricated two of my fingers as well, sliding them into Nora's pussy first before trailing them back towards her ass. I inched one finger in at a time, gently lubricating her ring of nerves. And all the while, I gauged her every move, every exhale. When she pushed back at my hand, three-fingers deep now, I knew she was ready.

I notched the tip of the plug against her opening. She tensed when I began to push it in. "Relax, baby. Breathe out." I clicked the remote and the plug vibrated to life. I dragged it against her clit a couple of times, before sliding it to her back entrance again. On her next exhale, I pushed it in again, this time until it was fully seated inside her. I caressed her lower back. "How do you feel?"

"Full," she exhaled. Her body quivered for me.

"Well, you're about to be even fuller."

I shifted behind and dragged my cock against her slit. I plunged my cock into her from behind and set a furious pace. The plug in her ass created an almost vise-like grip on my cock and the vibrations licking the underside of my balls had me seeing stars. It didn't take long to find our rhythm.

Her arms gave way beneath her after one particularly punishing thrust. She collapsed to the bed and cried out against the sheets. Ever the opportunist, I reached for the ribbon from her discarded corset. She gasped when I tugged her arms behind her and began to wrap her wrists with the silk strings, all without missing a stroke.

"Tell me now if this isn't okay." I breathed heavily.

"No! Keep going. Please." She threw her head back. "Please don't stop." I loved the way she begged.

I tightly bound her wrists, holding them to the small of her back as I continued to fuck her. Oblivion was just out of reach. Her muffled moans against the sheet had me rutting into her deeper, faster.

"Want more, baby?"

"Yes! God, please I want it all." I reached for the remote again and cranked up the intensity of the vibrations. "Fuck! I'm going to come," she shouted, chasing her orgasm.

"That's right." I reached one hand around her hips to flick her clit. "Fucking come for me, Nora." That was all it took to send her over the finish line.

Nora's orgasm rolled through her body like a riptide, the pulsing waves of her pussy pulling me under. Indescribable pleasure rioted through me as she clamped down on my cock, and I unloaded into the condom. We fell to the bed, her well-used body sagging beneath mine.

I rolled us to our sides, careful to keep the condom from slipping out of place. Even with the condom, I could feel our sweat and lube puddling on the sheet beneath us.

I untied her wrists, taking special care to caress every mark or indentation as I uncovered it. Next came the plug. I took my time removing it from her ass before setting it aside. I made a mental note to clean it later, as soon as I gained the feeling back in my toes. Beyond that, I kept my body connected with hers. I wasn't ready to let her go just yet. For fuck's sake, she was still twisted up in that sexy thong of hers.

She rested her head on my outstretched arm while I peppered her neck and shoulders with feather-soft kisses. God, I loved her body.

Who was I kidding? I loved her.

"Thank you," I said against her neck. So softly, I didn't think she heard me, so I said it again a little louder. "Thank you."

Her body shook with laughter.

"I'm afraid to ask what you're laughing at while my cock's still inside you."

"No, it's not that," she choked out between laughs. "I made a bet with myself before and I just won."

"What'd you bet?"

"Just that underneath the sweet and caring tea shop *bloke*, was a dirty-talking sex god." She used her internal muscles to squeeze my softening cock. The vise-like grip was enough to bring it back to life.

"Stay the night," I murmured against the top of her head.

"We'll see."

I smiled. We both knew she'd be staying. As it was, we were both already half-asleep. But judging by the moisture coating my dick and thighs, we'd have some cleaning-up to do before bed. The last thing either of us wanted for Christmas was a UTI. Plus, the only thing that could possibly make this night any better would be a shower with Nora. A wet, naked Nora.

"Stay forever."

"We'll see."

Chapter Nine

December 22nd

Nora

F ive days.

That's how long it'd taken to fall head-over-heels for Bowie Harrison. To be completely honest, I'd been falling for him for weeks now. Ever since I'd barged in on him (and his exposed penis) in the Miller family's bathroom. But it'd been the last five days of holiday events, late-night talks, and marathon sex sessions that cemented my feelings for the adorkable Brit.

The Twelve Days of Christmas? More like the Twelve Days of Dickmas. After the thorough dicking I'd received over the last week, there was no doubt in my mind that this year, I'd be on Santa's Naughty List. And it was all thanks to Bowie.

We'd spent the entire day after the Bachelor-XXX-Mas party at his place fucking round the clock. It'd started with me waking up to Bowie's head between my thighs, where he proceeded to lick me until

I screamed. I'd returned the favor later while cuddling on his couch, in between episodes of "The Great British Baking Show".

After he'd bent me over the kitchen counter and taken me from behind, he'd introduced me to his fruitcake, which was one, not a euphemism and two, nothing like American fruitcake. Fruitcake, as I knew it, had always been the dry, passive-aggressive holiday gift reserved for distant relatives. The ones you only kept up with on Facebook for "the sake of the family". Bowie's fruitcake might as well have been a living, breathing creature. It needed constant care. He kept his fruitcake moist by "feeding it" whiskey every few days, which was a holiday tradition I could get behind.

Later that night, I'd ridden him reverse-cowgirl style on the carpet by a roaring fire, much to Banger's dismay. Not only had I usurped her *daddy*; I'd also stolen her spot by the fire. The best part though, was we'd ended the weekend the same way we'd started it, snuggled together in Bowie's bed.

And then we'd done it again the next day. And the next. And the next. Which led to now; Bowie lazily pumping into me from behind, both of us on our sides, while I pressed my favorite vibrator to my clit.

He moaned. "Fuck, Nora. That feels incredible."

As I'd discovered, Bowie enjoyed toys just as much as I did. We'd taken turns experimenting with each other's bodies this past week, learning what made each other come. And that wasn't the only thing we'd taken turns with. Let's just say, my newly acquired butt plug had gotten quite the workout. Not only that, but the last time I'd stopped off at home to change my clothes and pack a bag – which could've been yesterday or three days ago, for all I knew – I'd made sure to grab a few more supplies. Of the battery-operated variety.

I positioned the toy lower, low enough for him to feel the vibrations every time he stroked in and out of me. Speaking of his strokes...

They were becoming faster and deeper by the second. His breathing quickened along with his strokes. I lifted my leg higher and draped it over his hip, opening myself up wider to him.

"I love the way you squeeze my cock," he rasped in my ear. "You take me so well."

It was his growl that made my inner muscles spasm around him. I loved bringing out this side of Bowie, the animalistic, primal part he reserved solely for the bedroom. I loved it. I loved h... *Nope, not going there.*

The slap of his balls against my ass mingled with the low hum of the vibrator. With one hand, I kept a firm hold of the toy. I used the other to grip the headboard and rock my body back against his. "Please, Bowie," I moaned breathlessly. "Please, make me come." My plea was futile. I knew I was only seconds away from release.

I'd barely gotten the words out before his free hand, the one not playing with my asshole, went to my throat. There was no real pressure, just enough to hold me in place while he fucked up into me.

Forget jewelry. I'd take Bowie's hand necklace over sterling silver any day.

It was the juxtaposition of gentle neck kisses and the firm pressure around my throat that sent me soaring over the edge. "Fuck Bowie," I gasped. He plunged into me two more times before seating himself fully inside and releasing a deep, guttural groan.

I let Bowie take care of the condom while I cleaned up and then, slipped on a pair of leggings, sans underwear. "That's not fair," Bowie groaned. I turned to find him leaning against the mountain of disheveled sheets and pillows, gloriously naked with his hands tucked behind his head. "I've got a dozen holiday orders to fill today and now the only thing I'll be able to think about is the fact that you're not wearing knickers."

"My *knickers*," I teased, "are all dirty."

"Oh no, how awful," he responded dryly.

"I've been living out of a duffel bag for like, five days." I picked up said bag and began stuffing it full of clothes. "I need to go home and do laundry sometime."

"You can do laundry here."

"Aren't you sick of me yet?" I meant it mostly as a joke. Hopefully, Bowie didn't pick up on the twinge of worry in my voice. Even though he was still working full-time, and up until yesterday I'd still had the dinner theatre show and my nannying responsibilities, we'd somehow spent every free moment together for going on a week.

On Monday, we'd celebrated the second night of Hanukkah with Leighton and her roommates. She was the closest thing to family Bowie had in LA and judging by the third-degree questioning I'd received during the Chrismukkah festivities, she was protective of her boss/pseudo-sibling. On Tuesday, Bowie had accompanied me to Sage and Olive's holiday pageant, a nightmare I wouldn't wish on my biggest enemy let alone on somebody I'm dating. Sage had been over the moon to see "the guy who talks funny and paints his nails" again, and I just about keeled over when Olive fist-bumped Bowie, her equivalent of those three little words. Yesterday, we'd gone ice-skating with Riley and Devin at L.A. Live and tonight, we'd made plans to see a midnight showing of "Scrooged" at the Nuart Theatre.

It was safe to say we'd moved well beyond the realm of "casual dating", and truthfully, that scared the shit out of me.

What scared me more was the way my body responded to him when he leaped across the bed, wrapped his arms around me and said, "Fuck no. I just got you. How could I possibly be sick of you?"

He nipped my breast through my bralette and slid his hands down my back until they cupped my ass and his fingers teasing my crease.

My eyes closed and my head lolled back on a moan. I'd let him play, but only for a minute. Any longer and I'd inevitably find myself naked again, which unfortunately, neither of us had time for this morning. Not to mention, my poor, sweet vagina needed a break.

I ran a hand through Bowie's copper curls, still slightly damp from his shower, and tightened my grasp. I used my fistful of hair to tilt his head back until he met my gaze. He licked his lips in wait. I pressed my mouth to his and used my tongue to tease open his lips. Only when I felt his fingers drift further south did I slip away from his grasp. He flopped face down on the bed with the same theatrics of a child throwing a temper tantrum. I laughed.

"Shouldn't you get going?" I asked. While Althea's was technically closed for the rest of the week, Bowie still had several catering orders to fill. It shouldn't have come as a surprise. Los Angelenos were goo-goo for gluten-free, holiday eats and treats.

"I told Leighton I'd be in at noon. Which means, I've still got…" He turned towards the clock beside the bed, providing me with a front-row viewing to his bare ass. "About twenty minutes." He wagged his eyebrows.

Just as I decided he was too cute to resist, and that my vagina could handle one more trip to Pound Town, my cell phone rang. I followed the sound out of the bedroom and down the hall, until I finally found the device buried beneath yesterday's jeans. Bowie had stripped them off me after dinner and gone down on me. Right there at the dining table.

My stomach dropped the second I saw Ali's name flash across the screen. *This is it*. This was the call I'd been simultaneously waiting for and dreading. "Hello?"

"Guess who wants to see you for a chemistry call back?" Ali asked. We both squealed like teenagers. Ali might've been my agent, one of the youngest agents in Hollywood in fact, but she'd also become my friend. Bowie entered the room, now clad in sweatpants, just as we reached the tail end of our squeal fest.

"Okay, okay. So, what's next?" When Bowie held up his hands, I pulled the phone away and mouthed, *I got a call back.* He pumped his fists into the air and launched into a victory lap around the room. Like a red-headed, freckle-faced Rocky Balboa. Damn, he was cute.

So cute in fact, that I realized I'd tuned out the first part of Ali's response. "...and I know they told you after the holidays, but everything's been moved up, so they need to see you tomorrow."

And just like that, I wasn't laughing anymore. My entire body stiffened. "Wait, what?" Bowie must've recognized the shift in my body language – or maybe the fear eclipsing my voice – because he ceased his celebratory lap immediately.

"The director had a scheduling conflict, so the entire production's been moved up two weeks," Ali repeated. "I know it's a fast turn-around and it's not what we were planning for, but they need to see you tomorrow."

"Tomorrow? Ali, I can't–"

"You haven't left town yet, right?"

"No, I'm here for the holidays. But I'm not ready. I can't..." I choked. My vision darkened.

"You can do this," she reassured me. "This is it, Nora. This is what we've been waiting for. I know it and you know it." Ali's voice became fainter and fainter, until it sounded like nothing more than garbled words under water.

Tomorrow? I can't be ready by tomorrow. I haven't read the new sides. I don't have any clean clothes to wear. What if there isn't parking? I can't–

"Breathe." Bowie's voice permeated the fog circling my brain. "Breathe, Nora," he repeated softly. When had he begun rubbing circles on my back? I sucked in a much-needed breath and let it out. Then another.

"Nora? Are you still there?" I turned my attention back to the phone in my hand. Ali was still talking.

"Yeah, sorry."

"I know this is overwhelming..." she said. That was putting it mildly. "And that there will be other jobs. But I also know that this is nothing you can't handle. You're so close, babe." I nodded while she spoke. She was absolutely right. There would be other jobs, but it wasn't every day a fat actor had a shot at a leading romantic role. I wasn't willing to let this one go.

"I know," I said softly. And then again, louder this time. "I know. Okay, send me the sides as soon as you can, and I'll get to it."

"You've got this, Nora."

As soon as we said our goodbyes, I gave way to the thoughts and fears and doubts tap-dancing across my mind. It didn't happen often, usually only with jobs or relationships I really cared about. I'd had them about Bowie when we'd first hooked-up. But they were doing damage now.

"Nora, is everything okay?" Bowie asked.

I readied myself for the pain I was about to cause for myself and Bowie. As far as I could tell, there wasn't any other option. I couldn't think about him right now. Maybe it would sound selfish, but I needed to focus on this. On me. If he really wanted to be with me, he'd understand. He'd have to. He was dating an actress now.

I evened my breath and turned to face the man I'd begun to think of as home. "I need to take a break."

Bowie

Somewhere in the last thirty seconds, Nora and I had taken a hard left from our own personal Hallmark movie and run face-first into my least favorite episode of "Friends".

"A break from what?" I swallowed. "From me?"

I was suddenly thankful that I'd put on pants. The only thing more uncomfortable than being vulnerable was being vulnerable in the buff.

"Yes. No." That cleared things up. "I don't know."

When I stepped closer, she pulled away. I held out my hand, but she drew hers away. This wasn't right. We'd finally found our rhythm these last few days, finally set a pace that worked for both of us, or so I thought. All that progress and now she wanted to take two steps back.

"What's going on?" I walked around the table to take a seat on the sofa. The same sofa I'd fucked her silly on (and over) for days on end. I patted the empty space beside me, and she took the hint, though I didn't miss the way she made sure to leave some space between us when she sat. "You got the callback. Isn't that what you wanted?"

"Of course, it is."

"Then what's the problem?"

"They moved the callback up to tomorrow."

Not ideal, but not impossible. From what she'd told me before, the callbacks were originally supposed to be held after the holidays. No wonder she was anxious. I reached across the couch to lace my fingers with hers. Her back stiffened, but she allowed it.

"Okay, I know that wasn't part of the plan. But –"

"Part of the plan? None of this was part of the plan." Her fingers tightened around mine to the point of discomfort, but I didn't say anything. "*You* weren't a part of the plan. *This* wasn't a part of the plan." She gestured between the two of us.

"This?" I asked.

"This. Us." She said it slowly, as if she were lecturing a child.

"I thought you liked *us.*" I stroked her tense knuckles. It was hard to believe that just an hour ago, she'd been laid out like a limp noodle in my bed. "You told me that *us* made your audition better."

She sighed. This one was a sigh of defeat. "I do. It did." She choked back a sob. My heart stopped when she turned her face and I saw the unshed tears clouding her eyes. "And I don't want to let it go."

"You don't have to." I brushed a fallen tear from her cheek. "We can do this together, just like last time. I can run lines with you, call in extra help at the shop. I know I have orders to fill, but I have some staff that's still in town for the holidays and I'm sure they'd be willing to lend a hand."

She was already shaking her head. "No. No. I have a job to do and so do you." She dropped my hand and jumped to her feet. When she disappeared into the bedroom again, I didn't know what to think. Was that the end of the conversation? She reentered the room a couple minutes later, this time with her duffel bag in hand.

"Are you leaving?" *Bollocks, is that my pitiful voice?*

"I was already leaving, remember?"

"But you'll be back, right?" When she didn't respond right away, I added, "We have that movie tonight."

"Bowie," she started. I didn't like the way she'd lowered her voice. It rang of the dreaded *"We need to talk"* sort of tone, one that I was all too familiar with. "I can't go to the movie."

Fight for her. "That's fine. How about I just come over tonight and we run through your lines?"

"I can't do that either." My chest all but cracked in half. *Please Nora, please don't push me away.* I stared at her, willing her to meet my gaze, even as she focused on the bag in her hands. "I just need some time."

"Nora..."

"Bowie, please." She looked up, her eyes piercing mine. "You remember how I told you I suck at saying what I mean when I mean it?" She waited for me to nod before continuing. "Well, this is one of those times. I want to be with you. I do. That's not what this is. I love..." She paused. The room grew suddenly quiet. I counted my heartbeats as I anticipated her next words.

Seven. "I". Eight. "Love". Nine. "You." Ten.

"I love being with you..."

Fuck me.

"...but I need some space. Just while I prepare for this callback. I can't rely on you, or anybody, to make *my* dreams come true. That's on me."

"But what if I want you to rely on me? I can do that for you. I can –"

"You *cannot* be my *everything*."

I stopped cold. She was right. For as long as I could remember, I'd been somebody's *everything*. I'd spent the better part of my adult life in relationships for one, two, three years at a time. I'd helped my partners apply for jobs, go back to school, start businesses even. I'd traveled with them and met their families, picked out furniture with them and indulged in their hobbies. And what did I have to show for it? What had being their *everything* gotten me?

Alone, that's what.

The slam of a cabinet shook away the hazy visions of Ghosts of Partners Past. Nora exited the bathroom, stuffing her toiletries bag into her duffel. *Don't let her run.*

"What about Christmas?"

Nora looked taken aback by the question. "What about it?"

"I thought," I stammered. "I thought maybe we'd spend Christmas together."

Her lips parted. "We can talk about it later. After the callback." She threw the strap of her bag over her shoulder. *This can't be it.* My heart rate skyrocketed as I followed her towards the front door. I'd be damned if I was going to let her leave without some concrete answers.

"And Riley and Devin's wedding?"

"Is still happening. Again, we can talk about all of this later."

"Nora." I rubbed the back of my neck raw. I had nothing left to lose at this point.

"What?" She turned.

"I love you."

She gasped. "Don't." She shook her head. "Don't say that just to get me to stay. Don't say that unless you mean it."

"I do." There wasn't a doubt in my mind. We might not have been together for long. Hell, we hadn't actually had the conversation of whether we were "together". But I knew what was in my heart. I could count the people I'd truly loved on one hand.

My mums, who yes, were in fact two people, but when combined, formed one powerful unit. My best mate, Killian. My mischievous wiener dog, Banger, though she wasn't technically a *person*. My name-sake, the late, great David Bowie. And one Nora Sanders, my purple-haired, dirty-mouthed, fat-bottomed girl. There wasn't a thing I'd change about her. Even now, when she was driving me positively mental, I loved her still.

With one hand, Nora held onto the bag draped over her shoulder. She wrapped the other around the back of my neck and crashed her lips down on mine. I gripped her waist, dragging her even closer. I could feel the heat radiating off her body, and I had no doubt she could feel my cock, hard as steel, pressing into her. I wanted nothing more than to drag her back to the cozy bubble we'd created these last few days, but I knew better.

We ended the kiss slowly, the opposite of how it'd begun. She traced my lips with her fingertips, and it took everything within me not nibble them the way I wanted to. "If you really love me," she started, "please respect what I'm asking for. I'm not running from this, from us. I just need to... do me for a minute." She searched my face and must've found the answer she was looking for, because she kissed me again. "I'll call you."

My heart never lied. If anything, my heart was too honest. Too open. But in that moment, I knew what Nora was offering. And what she was asking for in return.

It wasn't a goodbye. It was a promise.

***

"Right, mate. Run it by me one more time," Killian said. "Did you break up?"

"No, you wanker!" Leighton shouted over my shoulder and into the phone. Somehow, *wanker* didn't have quite the same effect when uttered in an American accent. "They're taking a break."

Thanks to Nora's untimely departure, I had in fact made it to Althea's by noon. Leighton, Hillary, and I had spent the past five hours baking, packaging, and ringing-up customers who had pre-ordered their holidays treats. It was a good thing I'd had them there to help, because otherwise, I'd have taken my frustration out in the kitchen. As it was, I'd still done a piss poor job of concealing my relationship turmoil and sadly, my first batch of peppermint biscuits had paid the price. Fortunately, my team had saved me from inflicting any further harm on baked goods.

We'd decorated tea cakes, boxed up tartlets, and crafted one elaborate gingerbread scene, all without massacre. It was when we were coming up on dinnertime and the final orders of the day that Killian called. His timing couldn't have been any better, even if his advice needed improvement.

"Taking a break?" Killian repeated. "What, like Ross and Rachel?"

Leighton rolled her eyes and turned to me. "You know, I don't want to say, 'I told you so,' but this never would've happened if you'd kept things casual like you said. It isn't too late to call Ben."

"Ben?" Killian's voice rang with confusion. "I thought her name was Nora."

She ignored him altogether. "Or I can give him your number."

"He doesn't need somebody else's number. He needs to go after Nora. That's what she wants."

"She literally said to give her space," Leighton spat into the phone. With the way they were arguing with each other – and ignoring me completely – I should've just handed it over to her.

"But that's not what she meant."

"Stop!" I'd heard enough. These were my two best friends, but suffice it to say, they didn't know my relationship better than I did. "Nora asked for some space, so that's what I'm going to give her…"

"Exactly," Leighton interrupted, smiling.

I held up a hand. "I wasn't finished. She asked for space, so I'm going to respect what she asked for, and give her that. Because I love her. I'm not giving up on her. I'm not giving up on us. I'm just giving her the space she needs."

Waiting for Nora would be no easy feat, but in my experience, great things were always worth the wait. I loved Nora. Those feelings weren't going away anytime soon. And while I wasn't exactly looking forward to going to bed alone tonight and waking up without her tomorrow, it was a small price to pay if it meant building a future together.

"You? Giving a girl space?" Killian chuckled and honestly, I couldn't fault him. I'd been a serial monogamist for my entire adult life and even just a brief look back at my relationships showed that I (maybe) had some boundary issues.

But there was one thing Killian had gotten wrong.

"No," I told him. "I'm giving *the girl* space."

Chapter Ten

December 24th

Nora

"Can I just say, I love you for not making me wear a taffeta nightmare? Best bride ever." I twirled in front of Riley and Devin's floor-length mirror, showing off the ways the emerald-green gown emphasized every one of my curves. "Seriously, are you sure you're okay with me looking this good at *your* wedding?"

Riley snorted. "I think I'll survive." She held up a pair of pearl drop earrings to my lobes. "But just saying, if I had this dress and your body, I think I'd wear this every day."

We both smiled. Hers was the smile of an eager bride-to-be, whereas mine was one of a woman playing a part. The part being *"Woman who fears she wrecked her budding relationship before it even began, because she hasn't heard from the guy in two days"*. It was my most challenging role yet.

"You could text him a picture, you know." She gave me a look that indicated she knew exactly where my mind had gone.

"No." I brushed off her words. The pearl earrings, too. This would look a lot better with something gold. "No, I told him I needed space."

"Right. To prepare for your callback, which was yesterday. And you nailed it!"

She was right. I had nailed it.

At first, I'd worried that the onslaught of emotions I'd been feeling since my talk with Bowie would negatively affect my callback, but really, they'd done the opposite. I'd channeled those fears and doubts and (gulp) love into quite possibly the most heart-wrenching callback of my life. And while that hadn't been what the role had called for, those emotions had added nuance to the character in a way that surprised me, my agent, and even the show's producers. Nothing was official yet, but I'd been told to have my rep on stand-by following the chemistry test, and that was a great sign.

"I know you at least want to tell him about how well the callback went," Riley pressed. "Don't pretend like you don't."

"Of course, I do. But how would that look?"

She handed me a petite pair of gold hoops. "What do you mean?"

"I told him I needed space. I told him not to call or text or come over –"

"And he hasn't." That was what surprised me most. While Bowie had agreed to respect my need for space, a part of me had still expected him to text me goodnight. Or send me a "break a leg" bag of cookies. Or call me to arrange Christmas plans. But he hadn't done any of that. And I was both impressed and disappointed by his restraint.

For fuck's sake, you finally found a guy who respects you and even that pisses you off.

"I don't know what's wrong with me." I slumped onto her bed.

"Nothing's wrong with you, Ra-Ra." She sat down next to me and draped her arm around my shoulder. "You're in love."

I wiped the runaway tear from my cheek. "That's the meanest thing you've ever said to me." I leaned my cheek on her shoulder and grumbled. "You and Dev make it look so easy."

Riley's laugh rang through the room. "Relationships are never easy, you know that." Her eyes met mine in the mirror. "But they're definitely a lot *easier* when it's somebody you like, as well as love. Somebody who listens to you, who respects you. Somebody who makes you laugh, but who also lets you cry. Somebody you want to be the last person you talk to before you fall asleep at night and the first person you see when you wake up." It might've been Riley stroking my shoulder, but all I could feel was Bowie. "Does that sound familiar?"

I sighed. "Crap. I'm a dumbass."

"That's okay," she said. "We've all been there." She takes my hand in hers before slapping something hard and cold into my palm. My phone. "I've found it's best to just tell them you've been a dumbass and apologize. Oral sex helps, too."

If all it took to sustain a healthy relationship were apologies and blow jobs, Bowie and I were set. He'd been so understanding of me and my needs thus far, I had no reason to believe that had changed. Right? No, now wasn't the time to overthink. Even with Riley looking over my shoulder, I typed out a quick text asking if we could meet up later to talk. We both agreed that that sounded a bit too vague or ominous, so I decided to call instead.

Bowie answered after the first ring. "Nora?"

"Bowie. God, it's so good to hear your voice." I swallowed every ounce of my pride. "I've missed you."

"I've missed you, too."

"Listen, I know-"

I was cut off by the sound of feet running up the stairs. Not two seconds later, Devin came rushing into the bedroom. "Turn on the news," they heaved, straining to catch their breath. "We've got a problem."

Riley grabbed the nearby remote and switched on the television. Aside from my mom and stepfather, Riley and Devin were the only people I knew who still paid for basic cable.

"Nora?" Bowie asked from the other end of the phone.

"I'm sorry, hold on a second. Something's going on."

Devin narrated the scene on screen. "There was a massive snowstorm in Big Bear last night and they're expecting more tonight. Roads are completely closed, so Milo's stuck at the cabin."

"Baby, what's wrong?" Bowie's endearment warmed my heart. It was the first time he'd called me anything like that outside the bedroom. Hopefully, it wouldn't be the last.

"Sounds like the caterer is stuck in Big Bear," I whispered into the phone before turning back to the TV.

I couldn't believe what I was seeing. Cabins and cars all along Highway 18, blanketed in fresh powder. Seeing as we'd had an unusually warm winter, nobody had forecasted a white Christmas for the neighboring mountain towns. Big Bear was only a couple hours' drive outside of the city, but everything I'd seen up until now, hadn't projected snow until almost mid-January.

Mid-January my ass.

"They're saying the soonest anybody's getting out of here is the 26th," Devin added.

"The 26th? But that's the day we're getting married." Riley's widened eyes reflected the panic in her voice.

"Sweetie," Devin said, "I don't think they're going to make it."

"No. No. No." Riley ran from the room, probably in search of her wedding checklist. As far as Riley was concerned, if it wasn't on the checklist, it didn't count. More than once, I'd seen her add something to the list she'd already completed, just for the instant satisfaction of being able to cross it off. Unfortunately, while Riley was great at handling other people's crises, she usually didn't budget time for her own. If the crisis wasn't on the list...

She came running back into the room moments later with her list. "Okay, it's all going to be fine. We'll just call another caterer." She wracked her fingers through her hair.

Devin took Riley's hand in theirs before she could do any real damage to her scalp. "Honey, it's Christmas Eve and this is Los Angeles. Nobody stays in LA for the holidays unless they're working, and if they're working, I don't think they'd be available for a holiday wedding."

Riley's shoulders crumbled. I turned away from the two of them.

"Bowie, we're kind of having a wedding crisis here. I'm going to need to call you back."

"Put me on speaker."

"What?"

"Put me on speaker, Nora."

I clicked the speaker button. "Devin? Riley?"

"Yes?" Riley sniffled.

"There's at least one chef left in LA." Bowie's voice echoed through the room. "Tell me what you need."

"We couldn't ask you to do that," Riley protested.

"It's done. Though I'll be honest, I'm much more of a baker. I hope you're okay with pasties and pudding."

Riley's face said it all. Pasties and pudding might not have been the wedding aesthetic of her dreams, but at this point, it was either that or Bagel Bites. Devin might put together a mean charcuterie board, but the three of us had the combined cooking prowess of a nineteen-year-old frat boy.

"We'd really appreciate it," Devin said. "I'm sure whatever you make will be perfect."

"Good. Now what do you need?"

Devin nodded their head towards the door and I took the hint. I took the call out into the hallway so they could continue to comfort Riley. "It's just me now."

Bowie sighed. "Hi."

"Hi." I took a second to gather my wits. "I know there's a lot that needs to be said and this isn't fair to ask for your help, but–"

"There will be plenty of time for us to talk, baby." *Baby.* My racing heart slowed at the sound of his even keel tone. "But for now, please tell me what you need."

"I need dinner and dessert for twelve, and I need it by the morning after Christmas."

"Done."

Bowie

I pulled up to the Miller house at a quarter to midnight. It was hard to believe it'd only been a month since Thanksgiving. I parked behind Nora's Nissan and used the rearview mirror to finger comb my curls while replaying our phone conversation from earlier in my head.

I'd been surprised to hear from her at all, let alone to receive a call on Christmas Eve. I'd done my best not to bother her the last two days, though I had texted both Riley and Devin to check on Nora's wellbeing. Technically, that wasn't going against what she'd asked of me. They'd both assured me that my girl was fine, just a bit stressed. About the callback, the wedding, and maybe also, about me.

I'd already decided to call her on Christmas if I didn't hear from her before then. Because what could she do then? Get angry about me wishing her a "Happy Christmas"? If she wanted space, fine. But I wasn't going to let her run.

After Nora's phone call, I'd rang Devin directly with my questions about preferences and food allergies. They'd also offered up their brother, Peter, to be my interim sous-chef while Leighton finished up holiday orders at the shop. I wasn't sure how much I could utilize his "two summers working at Mr. Waffle, Boston's favorite food truck", but an extra set of hands was better than nothing.

Headlights flickered behind me. I got out of the car to meet Devin and Peter when they pulled into the Millers' driveway.

"We almost lost the cake along the way," Devin said after they got out of the car. My eyes widened. I'd spent all afternoon decorating the two-tiered Black Forest masterpiece.

"Bugger off. Please tell me everything's alright."

"With the cake? Yes." Their lips quirked up. "Maybe not so much with Peter."

"What do you –"

Just then, a bare-chested Peter climbed out of the car, holding a compress of some kind to his forehead. No, not a compress. His balled-up t-shirt.

"What happened?"

"I don't want to talk about it." He rounded the back of the car. "The stupid cake is fine though. You're welcome."

Together, the three of us unloaded both cars. Following Nora's call, I'd handed off any final pick-ups of holiday orders from Althea's to Leighton so I could focus solely on planning and preparing Devin and

Riley's wedding feast. I'd finished most of the dinner prep while the cakes baked. Leighton would be bringing the rest of the food, as well as some chafing dishes and serving supplies, on the morning of. And even though the wedding was still thirty-six hours out, I'd thrown in some pastries for tomorrow, too. It was Christmas, after all.

Seeing as my arms were currently loaded up with cake boxes, I heard the front door open before I saw who opened it.

"Well, well. Bowie Harrison."

I recognized my ex-girlfriend's voice instantly. I'd had the fore-thought to let Kendall know a while back that I'd started dating Nora, and she hadn't seemed to care. We also hadn't spoken in a few weeks, so I hoped she didn't mind that I was here. She crossed her arms and leaned her body against the doorway. Why did it suddenly feel like she was guarding the entry to the castle?

"Our chef in shining armor," she teased.

"Kendall, Happy Christmas."

She pursed her lips. "My sister is getting married in two days, my mom is riding my ass about moving across the world, and you're dating a family friend. What's happy about that?"

These boxes just got a whole lot heavier.

"I'm just fucking with you. Here." She took the top two boxes out of my arms, immediately lightening my load. After we set everything down on the dining room table, I patted her shoulder.

"Thank you." She shrugged. It was a softer side of Kendall; one I wasn't used to. "You know, Devin and Peter are still unloading the car." She looked at me quizzically. "Peter has no shirt on." I wasn't blind. I'd peeped the six pack on Devin's brother. Which is why it didn't surprise me when Kendall smiled and took off like a bat out of hell.

From the dining room, I had the perfect vantage point of the entire downstairs. I spotted Riley and her father in the family room, crafting floral arrangements. Well, Riley was crafting floral arrangements. Mr. Miller was struggling not to prick his finger on the thorns. Mrs. Miller was currently pacing the kitchen, phone to her ear. From what I could pick up on, she was having some sort of linen emergency.

"I distinctly said, 'Hunter Majestic', Carol. Not 'Moss Majestic.'" I guess the food wasn't the only thing not going according to plan. I looked towards the living room and then the hallway to the garage, but nothing. No sign of Nora.

"Psst." I turned back to the family room and locked eyes with Riley. She pointed towards the stairs, and I swallowed my nerves.

When I reached the upstairs landing, I immediately noticed the light peeking beneath the bathroom door. *The scene of the crime.* It wasn't the light that called me in closer though, it was the woman washing her hands on the other side of the door. I positioned myself in front of the door and used both hands to grip the doorframe. It only took a few seconds before the door opened and Nora ran face first into me.

Fuck, what a sight for sore eyes.

She wasn't wearing an ounce of make-up, and she'd thrown her purple hair into a messy bun atop her head. The dark circles under her eyes matched my own. There was some comfort in knowing I wasn't the only one who'd had a *shite* time sleeping alone the last few nights.

"We've got to stop meeting like this." I smiled, my first in days.

"You're here."

"You said you needed me." And with that, she launched herself at me. She pinned me against the hall linen closet, though I quickly reversed our positions. I slid my hands up and under her hoodie and dragged them across the heated skin I found beneath. "I missed you, baby," I whispered against her lips.

"I missed you, too." I dove in for another kiss, but she stopped me, a finger to my lips. "I'm sorry I froze you out. I shouldn't have done it like that. But between the callback and everything that's been happening between us, I just felt overwhelmed."

"I understand why you did what you did." I kissed her fingertip. "And honestly, I'm glad you did."

"You are?" I longed to kiss the crease between her brows next.

"You were right. I'm not exactly the best with boundaries. I thought I needed to be somebody's 'everything' to get them to stay with me. Otherwise, I'd wind up where I started. Alone in an empty house."

She ran her fingers through my hair and cupped my face. "That's not true. You have Banger." I smiled weakly. "And your parents. And Leighton. And Killian." She brushed my face with kisses after each. "And me. You have me." She twined her arms around my neck and pulled my lips to hers again. Her tongue invaded my mouth and she ground her pussy down against my now throbbing cock. And as much as I wanted to pull her into the Millers' bathroom and bend her delectable body over the vanity, this wasn't the time and place.

A sudden cheer from downstairs had us pulling our lips apart. The sharp crack of a champagne cork followed shortly after. "What are they celebrating?" Nora asked. When the sultry sound of Eartha Kitt singing about yachts and convertibles reverberated up the stairs, I smiled against her lips.

"Happy Christmas, baby."

"Where did all this 'baby' talk come from?" She teased my lips with the tip of her tongue. I, in turn, raised one of my hands to her neck.

"Would you prefer 'sweetie'? 'Darling'? 'Goddess divine'?"

Her shoulders shook. "So many options. In that case... I'll stick with 'baby'. And how about you, boyfriend?"

"Boyfriend?" I liked the sound of that.

"Yeah. Or would you prefer 'honey'? 'Shnookums'?" She leaned in to whisper, "Or maybe, 'love'?"

My grip on her neck tightened. "Only if you mean it."

"I do." She tipped her head back to look at me, eyes colored in adoration. "I love you, Bowie."

"I love you, too."

Epilogue

Christmas Day

Nora

I t'd been a while since I'd had a sleepover, and I don't mean one of the naked variety. Last night, I'd enjoyed an honest-to-goodness, pre-teen style sleepover at the Millers' house. I'm talking a movie marathon, cozy couch cuddles, and late-night (early morning, really) s'mores in the backyard fire pit. And booze. Because alcohol made everything ~~nostalgic~~ a bit more fun.

Seeing as Kendall and Peter had disappeared together somewhere around 3 a.m., Riley and Devin had taken Kendall's old room and left Riley's room to Bowie and me. And as much as I'd wanted Bowie to put his candy cane deep in my stocking last night, there were some things you just didn't do in your best friend's childhood bedroom. That didn't mean we hadn't indulged in some holly jolly shower time this morning. We'd let the water run cold while Bowie ate me out in the tub, my leg thrown over his shoulder. The water only did so much to muffle my moans though, and I'd bitten my lip hard enough to draw blood.

After breakfast, an arrangement of pastries Bowie had thoughtfully brought over from Althea's, we all took turns making the obligatory "Merry Christmas" phone calls to our families. I'd be celebrating with my mom and stepdad when they returned from their cruise in January, but I did spend a few minutes on Zoom with my dad and his girlfriend's family. Her kids told me how much they loved the presents I'd sent for them, and surprisingly, we finished the call without any passive-aggressive comments about my hair, body, or profession.

A Christmas Miracle, for sure.

Bowie spoke with his moms and even passed the phone off to me for a few minutes. I fell in love with Tammy and Ann Marie at first talk. They politely extended an invite to their belated Christmas festivities in the U.K. come February. I told them I'd be honored to attend, so long as it worked with my schedule. I still hadn't heard about whether or not I'd booked the show. As soon as Bowie heard them utter the words, "bathtub photos", he'd snatched the phone away and darted off to the hall. Which was fine because I had another call I needed to make. One that was extremely time sensitive. Bowie's Christmas gift depended on it.

Several hours later, we all gathered around the Millers' Christmas tree. Discarded wrapping paper littered the floor and mugs of Devin's famous Peppermint Hot Schnapp-late covered every surface. Banger, whom Bowie had retrieved from his place this morning despite the lengthy drive, had snuggled-up next to the Miller family's Chocolate Lab, Zeke. They'd become fast furry friends in the span of a few hours.

"This is the best fucking fruit cake of my life," Riley said around a forkful of fruit cake.

"Riley Miller!" Genie chastised.

"Riley Miller *Edwards*, Mom." Riley cuddled back against Devin's chest and lifted another bite of fruitcake to her lips. "I'm just stating the obvious."

"It's the whiskey," I told her.

"Some people prefer rum, but my family's always made it with whiskey," Bowie added proudly, and rightfully so. This was unlike any fruitcake I'd ever tasted. Maybe he'd show me how to make it next year.

I sighed. *Next year.*

Later, while everybody else was busy decorating the yard for tomorrow's nuptials, Bowie pulled me aside. Rather than steal me away to make out like I'd expected, he handed me a small white box from his coat pocket. "Happy Christmas."

"What? You didn't have to get me anything."

"None of that now. That's what boyfriends do." He pressed his lips to my forehead. *Damn.* We'd (officially) been "boyfriend" and "girlfriend" for less than twenty-four hours and already, he had it down pat.

I lifted the box lid. I couldn't contain my smile when I saw what lay inside: a necklace with a key pendant, both gold. "What's this?" I teased, "The key to your heart?"

"The key to my house." The smile fell from my face. Not because I was upset, but because I recognized his offering for what it was. A huge step forward in our relationship.

"Are you serious?"

He took my hand in his. "I'm not asking you to move in with me tomorrow. Just saying that you're welcome in my house, whenever you please. I like having you there and I'd like to see more of you there in the future. Our future." He reached forward to wipe the moisture from my eyes. I hadn't even realized I was crying.

I'd been a fool to try and resist this man and his Hallmark-esque grand gestures.

I wrapped my hands around his neck, leaned down, and kissed him. Unlike most of our previous kisses, this one was soft and slow. It wasn't a precursor to anything more. No, this kiss was the main event.

"Thank you," I said, when we finally came up for air.

"You like it then?"

"Remember that whole thing I told you about not buying people jewelry?" He nodded. "Yeah, well forget all that. I can honestly say this is the best piece of jewelry I've ever received."

We walked hand-in-hand towards the back of the house, stopping briefly along the way to pet Banger and Zeke. "Oh! I got you something, too," I told him. "But it hasn't arrived yet."

"That's okay." He winked, melting any remnants of frost that had previously covered my heart. *Lord, I sound like Scrooge.* "I'm not going anywhere. Besides, we've got a wedding to prepare for."

Boxing Day

Bowie

The Millers threw one hell of a party. Devin and Riley's wedding had gone off without a hitch, or rather, without any more hitches.

We'd slept over at the Millers' house for the second night in a row, so we could get an early start this morning, though calling it sleep was a bit generous. I was absolutely knackered, and I had the bloodshot eyes to prove it. Mrs. Miller's "Hunter Majestic" tablecloths were thankfully delivered bright and early, around the same time Leighton arrived to help me finish prepping the food. We'd been given full domain over Mrs. Miller's kitchen, which according to Riley, was the highest of honors.

Together, Leighton and I had prepared the wedding feast – prosciutto and ricotta cheese crostini, glazed peach skewers, mushroom and Gruyere tartlets and finally, individual chicken pot pies, made with homemade pie dough, naturally. The hours flew by as I jammed pan after pan into Mrs. Miller's small, electric oven. I'd truly been spoiled by my industrial convection oven.

By the time four o'clock rolled around, things were looking up. Really, there was no reason for me to attend the ceremony – it was after all, a small gathering of family and close friends – but Leighton had insisted. She all but pushed me up the stairs to change into my suit and tie, insisting that I be there for Nora. And bloody hell, I was glad she had.

Nora was a vision. When I watched her walk down the aisle, a pathway of rose petals sprinkled between two rows of chairs, I could've sworn my tongue fell clean out of my mouth. She'd traded her usual crop tops and cozy sweaters for an off-the-shoulder, dark-green gown. One that flowed down her body like liquid silk, clinging to every dip and curve along the way. It was the slit down the side of one leg exposing her tattooed thigh that had me readjusting my suddenly too-tight pants. That and the golden key necklace resting between her cleavage.

After the ceremony, we all sat down to dinner. Well, they sat down to dinner. Leighton and I eventually joined them, but only after making sure everybody had gotten enough to eat. We toasted Devin and Riley, laughed as Mr. Miller fumbled his speech because he was crying too hard, and tore up the makeshift dance floor.

Later, while everybody was enjoying their second piece of cake, Nora dragged me into the living room. I'd been hoping for some time alone with her all day, especially if that time involved me sliding my hand up the slit in her skirt to see what she was wearing – or not wearing – underneath. But she had other things in mind.

"I got it," she said, excited but dazed.

"Got what?"

"I got the part."

"Oh my god!" I gathered her in my arms. "That's amazing, baby. Congratulations!"

"They want me to start January 3rd. I can't believe it."

"Believe it." I ran my palms up and down her arms. "You worked hard for this." Whether she needed a shoulder to cry on, a cheerleader to wind her up, or a friend to give her a wee bit of space, I'd be there. Even if I didn't love the sound of that last one.

"Thank you." She brushed a kiss to my jaw and another to my cheek before landing exactly where I wanted, with her lips on mine. Just as I parted her lips with my tongue, she pulled away. "Uh uh, none of that right now."

"Come on, let's go upstairs."

A knock rapped at the door.

"Sorry, you'll have to wait until later." There was a devilish glint to her smile. *What is she up to?*

"Why's that?"

"Your Christmas gift just arrived."

I pointed towards the Millers' front door, and she nodded. I don't know what I expected to find when I opened the door, but it certainly hadn't been Killian. To say I was gobsmacked to see my best friend since childhood, the bloke I called my brother, waiting on the Millers' doorstep, would be an understatement.

"There's the lucky sod." Killian's six-foot-two frame crowded the doorway. His disheveled clothing and six o'clock shadow were no match for his rugged good looks. *Damn you, you beautiful bastard.* "Don't I get a hug for dragging my arse across the globe?"

I blinked away the moisture clouding my eyes and threw my arms around him. He hugged me back, like a soldier who hadn't seen his family in years, even though it'd only been nine months. Up until now, Killian had always been my connection to home. A lifeline to call on for comfort. That would never go away. Killian would always be my family, but in the last few weeks, my family had grown exponentially.

"What is *he* doing here?"

Speaking of family...

Leighton glowered at Killian. "*He* is here to see his best mate," Killian retorted. "Are you that pushy employee, then? Payton?"

"It's Leighton." Steam practically rolled off her shoulders. When she crossed her arms under her chest, I didn't miss the way Killian eyed her breasts. That seemed like a disaster in the making.

"Fancy a pint?" I patted his chest.

"Always."

I wrapped my arm around Nora's waist and dropped a kiss to the crown of her head. She didn't know it yet, but I was already brainstorming all the ways to thank her properly later this evening. Tomorrow, too. My gratitude had no bounds.

As we rejoined the others, I marveled at how a day that'd started in chaos could end in love. I saw it in the way Devin longingly stared at Riley, even as she frolicked across the yard after one-too-many glasses of champagne. I saw it in the way Mr. and Mrs. Miller held each other when they danced long after we'd turned off the music. I saw it in my best mate, who'd flown halfway around the world just to see me.

And of course, I saw it in Nora. When she hugged me, kissed me, laughed with me, stroked my hair, as she was doing now. The only difference was, with Nora, I didn't just see the love. I felt it, too. More than that, Nora had given me the one thing I'd been missing since moving to Los Angeles. The thing I'd longed for since losing my nan and moving so far from my family.

She'd given me a home.

I was finally home for Christmas.

The End

Thanks for Reading!

T hank you so much for taking a chance on a new indie author and reading *Meet Me in Los Feliz*. I hope you fell for Bowie & Nora, just like I did!

Stay tuned for Killian & Leighton's story in 2023.

If you liked this novella, please let me know and share with others by leaving a review on **Amazon** or **Goodreads :)**

Acknowledgments

Full disclosure, I wrote my Academy Award acceptance speech when I was sixteen. Obviously, some people, places, and things have changed since then, but seeing as this might be my one shot, let's see if I can get through this without crying (or without them playing me off).

Thank you to my beta, ARC, and sensitivity readers for their love and feedback. Especially, TEAM BETA – Natalie, Alanna, Kathryn, MK, Aaron, Sarah, Bree, Becky, & Laura! You don't know how much I treasured your feedback, and I promise that someday, I'll figure out how to properly use a dialogue tag.

To my amazing cover artist, Julie Olivia, thank you for bringing my vision to life (and for making Nora's hips bigger when I asked).

I'd like to thank my parents, because I wouldn't be who I am today without them. Mom, you've always been my number one fan, reader, and unofficial editor. Dad, I treasure your love and support... Maybe someday, you'll be able to remember the title of my book when you recommend it to people at the grocery store.

Shout out to the Bridesmaids chat, the Real Housewives of Alameda group, All Write, All Write, All Write team, and my Voxer Pod Squad - you all know who you are and how much you mean to me. Thank you for the hours of input, advice, memes, and Tiktok videos.

Special thanks to Romancelandia - from the authors to the bloggers, publishers, and more - for welcoming Boobies & Noobies into the fold nearly five years ago. Before starting the podcast, I had no idea that a community like this existed. I'm so grateful to be a part of it.

Lastly, thanks to everybody who has supported Boobies & Noobies over the years. The authors I've interviewed, the friends (and sometimes strangers) who shared their first romance read with me, the publicists/assistants/etc. who continue sending me books to read (even though I'm *shite* at writing reviews), and of course, the listeners. THANK YOU for getting me here. I hope we continue this journey together.

Oh, and just in case I never get the chance, I'd like to thank the Academy.

About the Author

By day, Kelly Reynolds works primarily as a freelance writer, professor, and author's assistant. By night, she hosts the romance novel review podcast, Boobies & Noobies. She's ghostwritten two previous novellas, but *Meet Me in Los Feliz* is her debut self-publication.

She currently lives in Portland, Oregon. When she isn't writing, you can often find Kelly eating her way through hole-in-the-wall restaurants, sampling cider at the nearest brewery, or bingeing the latest season of "Top Chef".

Keep up with Kelly on social media @realkellyrey and on her website: https://www.kellydaniellereynolds.com/

Keep up with Boobies & Noobies on social media and on our website: https://boobiesandnoobies.com/

Printed in Great Britain
by Amazon